"I don't think of you as Daryl's poor grieving widow.

"I see you as a woman with needs and wants."

"I don't have those kinds of feelings anymore."

"Then what I'm about to do won't affect you at all . . ."

Before she could move or speak he had covered the small distance between them and was pushing her against the closet door, holding her there with his body. He lightly claimed her lips with his, testing her, tasting her like a fine wine . . . She did not object when his tongue caressed the inside of her mouth.

He lowered his head to nibble kisses and whisper soft, half-intelligible words into her neck, but she moved too fast, finding her legs and strength of will at last.

"Get out."

Dear Reader:

After more than one year of publication, SECOND CHANCE AT LOVE has a lot to celebrate. Not only has it become firmly established as a major line of paperback romances, but response from our readers also continues to be warm and enthusiastic. Your letters keep pouring in—and we love receiving them. We're getting to know you—your likes and dislikes— and want to assure you that your contribution does make a difference.

As we work hard to offer you better and better SECOND CHANCE AT LOVE romances, we're especially gratified to hear that you, the reader, are rating us higher and higher. After all, our success depends on *you*. We're pleased that you enjoy our books and that you appreciate the extra effort our writers and staff put into them. Thanks for spreading the good word about SECOND CHANCE AT LOVE and for giving us your loyal support. Please keep your suggestions and comments coming!

With warm wishes,

Ellen Edwards

Ellen Edwards
SECOND CHANCE AT LOVE
The Berkley/Jove Publishing Group
200 Madison Avenue
New York, NY 10016

Second Chance at Love

MIRAGE
MARGIE MICHAELS

A
SECOND CHANCE AT LOVE
BOOK

MIRAGE

First edition published July 1982

First printing

"Second Chance at Love" and the butterfly emblem are trademarks belonging to Jove Publications, Inc.

Printed in the United States of America

Second Chance at Love books are published by
The Berkley/Jove Publishing Group
200 Madison Avenue, New York, NY 10016

MIRAGE

CHAPTER ONE

HONEY CALDWELL TURNED the ignition of her bright orange-red Bronco to "off" and stepped out of the black vinyl driver's seat that seemed to act as a solar collector for the sun's hot summer rays.

"Hey, where are you going?"

"To find a cool spot." She tossed an answer back to the plump, vivacious brunette who still occupied the Bronco's passenger seat and continued on, heading for the grassy area that bordered the closed postal building. In Pahrump, Nevada, in the middle of summer, there was no cool spot, but the grass looked more inviting than the sand that surrounded it. Though its springtime greenery had faded to a scorched brownish-tan, she sank down upon it gratefully and drew her long bare legs in closer to her body. She pressed against the side of the building to take full advantage of its meager pre-noon shade.

She shaded her large hazel eyes from the sun's glare. The doors of the post office were closed for the ten thirty to eleven o'clock break when mail was placed in the private boxes in the lobby and the few postal workers hastily gulped cups of coffee.

1

Honey let her eyes wander with a sort of detached
interest to the dirt parking lot next door where even now
the conglomerate of dusty pickups, station wagons, trail
bikes, and tractors were pulling in for the day's mail.
People usually came at least fifteen minutes before the
building was to reopen. The enforced waiting was an
excuse to pass the time before lunch.

"Waiting for your mail, Honey?"

"Not today. I'm waiting to meet someone." She nodded to the owner of the café down the street, who, coffee
and doughnut in hand, took a break every day about this
time to walk to the post office and gossip with his friends.
Honey knew his habits because she came every day, too.
But not to get her own mail, as he'd suggested. Her
portion of the postal box shared with her mother-in-law
was always small and mostly junk mail. She'd stopped
all personal correspondence when Daryl died. It had
seemed easier at the time not to have to relive his accident
over and over again in writing, and now eighteen months
later, she found she had very little to say to people she
and Daryl had once been so close to. It was as if she
was an entirely different person with no link to her past
except her name and some unfinished business that only
one person could help her complete.

The real reason for her being here, beyond collecting
her mother-in-law Pauline's mail, came back to her and
she looked at her watch again. Ten more minutes...

The thermometer jutting out at a right angle from the
crumbling adobe wall taunted her with its 110-degree
reading. The desert heat was suffocating in spite of the
shade, bathing her in a fine film of moisture through the
thin cotton top and shorts she wore. The heat coupled
to anticipation was making the wait intolerable. Normally
she was a patient woman, but she had waited so long to
meet Turner Jameson.

"Turner...Turner...Turner." She said his name
aloud, under her breath, trying to visualize what he might
be like. He had been born and raised in Pahrump and
had been a good friend of her husband's many years ago.
From the two letters he had written in answer to hers,

she knew that he was now a Bureau of Land Management official and, of all the lucky things to happen, *he* was being sent to investigate the problem of the many abandoned mines that were hidden under this part of the Nevada desert, one of which had caved in on her husband Daryl and killed him.

She sensed that he would be courageous and kind. After all, it would take a courageous man to postpone the planning and development of the large parks system proposed for the area in order to *do* something about the mines. Some of the other people intimately involved with the work on the park didn't seem to care that the very people they were building the park for could be hurt or even killed if the mine problem wasn't taken care of. But Turner Jameson would *care!* And she had pinned her hopes on him, the man she almost felt she knew. He would be no bureaucrat like so many of the others she had written to and received no answer from. Born and raised in Pahrump, he would be a common man, and she could imagine him driving up in a Jeep or a truck, wearing the Levi's and denim or western shirt that was practically a town uniform and a wide brimmed hat to shade his nose from the sun.

Honey looked up to the sound of a high-powered engine expectantly, her face falling in disappointment as she saw the brand new silver smoke-colored Mercedes pull into the mail truck's reserved parking spot. Who ever the man behind the wheel was, it was not Turner Jameson. It was probably another out-of-town real estate broker come to get an advance look at the town. Land in Pahrump was suddenly very attractive to speculators. The proposed government park and recreation facility— within an hour's drive of the night life of Las Vegas— made it so. Pahrump had been teeming with visitors lately, now that work was to commence on the park within a few weeks time. And this visitor who emerged from his Mercedes seemed to be even more impressed with his own importance than most.

The tall, lean, expensively dressed man looked to be out of the ordinary even from the usual out-of-towners she had just likened him to. There was an aura of superiority about him that was almost tangible. Like several others, she watched him curiously, her eyes drawn to him by the aggressive magnetism that was apparent in his every movement, yet that he didn't appear to be conscious of. His stride, as he walked to the post office door, was purposeful. He moved with the grace of a young athlete, belying the few flecks of silver at the temples of his otherwise well-styled mahogany-brown hair.

He tried the door, and finding it locked, rapped on it loudly and frowned at his watch as if the time piece was somehow at fault for his delay.

"Excuse me, but do you have the correct time?"

She brushed a stem of grass from her legs and met the object of her speculations at the door, her interest mingled with embarrassment that he had caught her staring at him.

"Why yes, I do," she said. "It's ten forty-nine, but the post office is closed until eleven, I'm afraid."

The stranger ran one finger down a long, aquiline nose, wiping the moisture from his skin. His brows furrowed, adding to the already rugged, interesting character of his angular face that did not quite fit in with the image his clothes presented. He rattled the door again ineffectually.

"I wasn't aware of that. I've been on the road for several days and I was hoping to check on some forwarded mail before an appointment."

She crossed her arms philosophically and gave a long suffering nod towards the building. "Unless you have an extra ten or fifteen minutes to wait, then I'd suggest coming back sometime before five. I've lived here for three years and I've never known them to open early. I've resigned myself to waiting."

"Unfortunately I don't have the time to wait today," he said matter of factly. "If I had the time I'd try to talk you into going somewhere, preferably with air conditioning, for something tall and cold to drink while we both wait." His eyes took in the length of her, his gaze direct and unabashed, a mental caress to her skin. A look of regret crossed his face as the sound of muffled footsteps and jangling keys diverted his attention back to the front door.

Honey moved away a little from his disconcerting nearness and tried to suppress a smug smile. With the silver Mercedes and the money it implied, he might well be granted special favors in other circles, but he would need more than money and his admittedly virile good looks to breach postmistress Cora Mae Blanchard's private citadel. Cora Mae was notoriously bad tempered with early bird postal patrons.

She voiced her skepticism. "I'd be wary if I were you. I don't think you're going to get in."

"Oh, I think I might." He smiled at Cora Mae. "You see, I used to live here a long time ago. Cora Mae and I were friends, and I think she'll be so happy to see me back, even though it's just on business and only temporarily. She'll let me bend a few rules, I trust, when she learns I'm supposed to meet someone here and could miss them if I'm in the middle of her usual crowd."

It couldn't be! Honey's eyes widened and she touched the sleeve of his dark blue silk shirt timidly. "It's probably a coincidence, but I was supposed to meet someone here at eleven, someone who used to live here and who's in town on business. But I was expecting...that is...you wouldn't be...you couldn't be Mr. Turner Jameson, could you?" Her head shook from side to side hopefully as his nodded yes.

"Oh." She stared up at him towering above her, dumbfounded, her mind taking its own sweet time to assimilate how very different the real man was from her mental image of him.

"Something wrong?" he asked her without a trace of surprise.

"You're not what I expected." She blurted out the explanation.

"I *was* wondering how you planned to recognize me,

though if you hadn't figured it out for yourself by the time I'd gotten my mail, I'd have told you."

He slipped into the open door that Cora Mae held for him, adding as he disappeared around the corner and out of sight, "You're exactly as I had you pictured."

Honey was left to collect her wits—and her friend Teresa alone. "You didn't prepare me for *this*..." She pointed to the Mercedes. "Or for him. I thought you said he reminded you of Daryl?"

Teresa shrugged unconcerned. "He did when he left, though you have to understand that he left here, let me see, maybe fifteen years ago when he would have been eighteen or nineteen years old and I would have been ten or eleven. He and Daryl were the same age, their parents both owned some land and raised alfalfa, though Turner's not as much as Daryl's. They went around together, did the same things. He was sort of the same..." She stopped mid-sentence. "But he sure isn't now! I wouldn't have even recognized the man if we hadn't just been talking about him. He's coming over," she whispered. "And that's the best-looking man I've seen since...come to think of it, that may be the best looking man I've *ever* seen. I can't believe he lived here and I let him get away."

Honey cleared her throat meaningfully, hoping Teresa would control her oftentimes one-track mind and runaway mouth before Turner joined them.

"You've changed." Teresa pointed out the obvious without any welcoming preliminaries.

"So have you, and for the better I might add. I can remember you as a little girl with glasses and a pony tail who used to follow me around."

Teresa laughed and climbed into the Bronco, obviously flattered to be remembered. "That was me. If you're going to be in town long, we'll have to get together and talk over old times."

"Good idea. Maybe after the meeting."

Honey sighed thankfully at his polite reminder, wondering how she would have pried Teresa away otherwise, and slid behind the wheel.

"I'll follow you," he said.

The Mercedes roared into life behind them as they left the post office and turned onto the highway, heading out of town.

"Do you know if he's staying very long?" Teresa asked eagerly.

"I don't know." Honey answered without taking her eyes from the road ahead. "I imagine he'll want to stay a few days, long enough at least to look at a couple of the mines he's going to close. I think he'll be able to persuade people to wait on the park development until the mines are closed though, don't you think? He strikes me as the kind of man who's used to getting his own way. I'm glad I'm going to be working *with* him rather than against him."

Teresa sighed wistfully. "I don't care about working with him. I'm pea green with envy that you're going to be living with him. He did accept your invitation to stay at the Caldwell house didn't he?"

Honey glanced up into the rearview mirror catching a glimpse of his face, and then swerved sharply to avoid hitting a bewildered jack rabbit on the side of the road, sending a spray of sand over the cactus and sagebrush before she resumed her proper position on the narrow strip of asphalt.

"Honey?"

"Yes . . . I mean no, he's not going to be, as you put it, living with *me*. The house is huge, more a hotel than a house really, and with more than enough rooms with only Pauline and me living there. It's the logical place for him to stay."

"Pauline won't like it," Teresa said. "Your mother-in-law is bound and determined to keep you romantically uninvolved and a widow forever."

"Good, then we're of the same mind," Honey quipped. "For heaven's sake, Teresa, the man's going to be visiting for a few days, he's not moving in for the rest of his life, and, in any case, he's probably married or otherwise attached."

"He couldn't be." Teresa was confident. "No woman in her right mind would let that one out of her sight. If he were mine, I'd keep him under lock and key."

"You're being dramatic. He's just a man." She made a right-hand turn onto a dirt road, forcing herself to keep the Mercedes, which was now enveloped in dust, in sight, though she had an almost overwhelming urge to put some distance between them.

"A no doubt rich and for sure good-looking man..." Teresa added hopefully, clasping her hands together in mock prayer. "And one who is lonely and in need of a deep relationship with a slightly plump country girl."

Honey laughed as she pulled into a graveled driveway, showering rocks every which way from beneath the tires.

"You'd better give up on that dream my friend," she warned.

"Give up? I haven't even begun to work at it yet."

Turner pulled in alongside of them. The unimpressive squat mobile home they'd stopped next to served both as house and command post for the local Search & Rescue Commander Gerald R. Wade.

"This is the place?" Turner asked as they met on the path.

"This is it. Come on, I'll introduce you to everyone."

Honey hid a grin as Teresa linked her arm with Turner's and pulled him along initiating a monolog of small talk.

"Hello. Mr. Jameson? Glad to meet you at last." Gerry's big booming voice was warm. He held out a hand to Turner which was grasped in an equally firm grip.

"I'm a relative newcomer to the valley only having lived here six years," Gerry continued, "so I didn't have the pleasure of knowing you before, but it sure gives me pleasure to welcome you back. From what Honey's been telling me, you could be our salvation."

Turner looked surprised and Honey spoke up quickly. "I told them about the investigation you plan to conduct. Of course now that you're here, you can tell them the details yourself." She turned to Gerry. "Speaking of which, isn't it time to begin the meeting?"

"Well, I *had* planned to serve lunch to Mr. Jameson and a few of the officers beforehand, but it looks like everyone has jumped the gun and gotten here early." He added for Turner's benefit, "Everyone has been very anxious to meet you. Besides..." he winked conspiratorially to Honey, "he doesn't look to me to be dangerous enough to have to feed before the meeting. So if it's okay with everyone, why don't we get on with the meeting and save our indigestion until after?"

The group around them tittered appreciatively. Gerry's luncheon/meeting combinations were infamous, a liking for his brand of fire-hot cuisine an acquired taste. He'd been known to subdue the toughest adversary with nothing more than a bowl of his home-cooked chili, and he saw nothing wrong with stacking the deck in his favor by serving the lunch *before* an important meeting in which the guest speaker might be liable to disagree with him.

He motioned them into the next room which was used exclusively as a small auditorium of sorts, being filled with folding chairs and encompassing the entire triple width of the mobile at one end, and seated himself behind a desk that faced his thirty-member audience. Turner took a seat beside him and waited for him to speak.

"First of all, I'd like to welcome you all to this special meeting of the Pahrump Search & Rescue Organization." He looked over the people in the room, taking note of a few nonmembers among the familiar faces. "There are problems connected with this proposed park that we, as a Search & Rescue organization, would like to see worked out before the public is admitted to the area, in fact, before actual work begins on the project."

Everyone looked at Turner, expecting a favorable nod of the head or an approving murmur similar to everyone

else in the crowd, but none was forthcoming. He opened
a briefcase and withdrew some papers instead, his attention on whatever was written there. He rubbed a hand
over an increasingly worried brow.

"We are a strictly volunteer organization," Gerry emphasized. "We get most of our funds from an annual
fireworks sale, and we are hard pressed at times to furnish
what volunteers we do have with the necessary equipment
and training. When this development begins, we will
have more land to cover and more people to concern
ourselves with. Much of the land to be used for the park
is potholed with abandoned mines, never claimed or
filed, with rotting timbers and unshored tunnels, all just
waiting for the inexperienced visitor to fall into. We are
bound to have accidents, and since last year, we have
fewer trained people to undertake rescues of that type,
and no one local to train anyone else."

For a second he looked to Honey with compassion
and she felt the familiar stab of pain that always presented
itself whenever the mines were mentioned. She swallowed the lump in her throat, reminding herself that at
least now, thanks to Turner Jameson, no one else would
run the risk of being hurt by them.

"We've all written more letters to the government than
I can count, but before the park was proposed, no one
seemed to care much. Now, thanks to the continued and
persistent efforts of our Vice-Commander Honey Caldwell, we've been fortunate enough not only to have a
representative come and conduct an investigation, but to
have one who, having lived in Pahrump for many years,
is favorable to our cause as well. So I'd like at this time
to personally thank Mrs. Caldwell for her assistance and
extend a warm welcome to Bureau of Land Management
official Turner Jameson."

The polite applause quieted as the tall, impeccably
dressed man stood and faced his audience, his heavily
lashed brown cyes meeting Honey's at once, drawn there
magnetically, his expression slightly accusing and un-
certain. He paced in front of them, a man more confident

with actions than words, yet when he spoke it was with
self-assurance and without faltering.

"As Mr. Wade stated, I am here in my official capacity
to investigate claims that certain abandoned mines found
on property soon to be open to the public are dangerous.
From what Mrs. Caldwell has been telling me in her
letters and from what Mr. Wade says today, I understand
that some of you would like to see work postponed until
the mine problem is somehow corrected."

"That's right, Mr. Jameson." Gerry stepped in. "We
all feel strongly about that."

Turner gave him a cold stare. "I appreciate your input,
however one man's opinion does not make a concensus.
Frankly, I've spent the last several days contacting other
groups with interest in this valley who hold an opposite
opinion, who feel that there are adequate warnings on
the known mines as it is, signs, fences, that sort of thing."

Surprised and discontented whispers rumbled through
the crowd. This was the man who had come to help
them? Honey ignored the whispered questions that came
her way and sat up straighter in her seat, straining to
hear each word that he spoke.

"I have been told . . ." Turner continued, "that some
of the accidents reported in the past two years were
caused by people who purposely disregarded the posted
'no trespassing' and warning signs and who, in fact, had
to scale fences to reach a mine and its adjoining tunneling. In the first place, whatever is done or not done with
the mines, there can be no hope of putting a twenty-four-
hour guard around each known mine for security. Nor
can there be enough money to fill in every over-sized
gopher hole and erosion in this desert to save a handful
of reckless people from their own stupidity."

"Stupidity?!" Honey rose from her folding chair in
protest, not able to contain herself or believe what he
was saying. "Of all the accidents, six of which resulted
in death, *none* that I can recall was caused by stupidity."
She counted them off on her fingers. "There was a child
who wandered away from camp, an old man picking

wild flowers, a couple of teenage lovers whose only fault was that they weren't aware their car was parked on some unshored tunneling, a lost hiker and..." She faltered, biting her lower lip to regain control. "... a professional mine rescue team member who tried to rescue one of them. *You* should know that." Her chest rose and fell with the suppressed emotion.

"I am here to conduct an *investigation*, Mrs. Caldwell," he replied softly. "What I may believe and what I can prove are two entirely different things."

"Prove?" she echoed. "What do you need in the way of proof? If you need personal experiences, we all have them, at least those of us who have ever been involved in a mine rescue and felt the anguish, the fear, and the sense of frustration and helplessness that goes hand in hand with it. Beyond that we have collected a petition signed by a substantial number of citizens who want this project put on the back burner for awhile..."

"A substantial number translates as what, Mrs. Caldwell? And where is this petition? Can I see it? I'll need more than verbal hysteria to convince anyone, including myself, that what you claim has any basis in fact. Give me facts I can use! I need a clear picture of just where these mines are, how many of them there are, what kind of condition they are in, and so on. I have no way of knowing whether the accidents you speak of were the result of actual mine conditions that would present a significant danger to the general public or if these accidents were the result of negligent irresponsibility and unprofessionalism on the part of both victim and would-be rescuer."

He appeared unconcerned that he had alienated his audience, or that Honey still stood, deathly pale and motionless, staring at him in disbelief from the middle of the room.

"I don't know what you've been led to believe, but I have not come here to close the mines. At this time, we're not even sure who *is* responsible for either their closure, if deemed necessary, or their upkeep. Further, as I've just stated, I'm not sure the mines present a problem of the magnitude I was led to believe. What I am here to do, what I will do, is conduct a thorough investigation and make an objective decision based on the facts. When that's done, I'll let everyone know the results and we can take things from there."

Honey felt Teresa's restraining hand on her arm urging her to sit down. "Come on, Honey. Don't let it get to you. It's all right."

But it wasn't. No one who had ever known Daryl could have considered him negligent or unprofessional. Meticulously careful of both equipment and procedure, he had taught climbing classes, and had been on call with the police department for all difficult mine rescue work for years. And yet that professionalism and experience hadn't helped save his life when several tons of earth fell in on him and the victim he was trying to save from a rotting silver mine. No! She refused to be hushed!

Her voice was trembling as much as her body when she interrupted Turner's final comments. "Mr. Jameson, I can show you as many deathtraps as you need to see. I can keep you here forever and not run out of things to show you or facts to feed you. I've made a study of it for the past eighteen months and..." She paid no attention to, in fact did not even hear the gavel that Gerry tapped onto the desk, louder and louder.

"And I think it's time to call an end to this particular meeting." His deep baritone finally filtered through to her mind. "As Mr. Jameson says, there's still a lot of work to be done. We can all help by offering our time and our support, as well as any other information concerning the mines to Honey Caldwell who has, so graciously..." he emphasized the word, "...offered to show Mr. Jameson the mine locations. Any of you who can give her a hand with this task please see Teresa Stanley our secretary after the meeting. I think that's all for now; we will be getting in touch with all of you with progress reports as time goes on. Thank you all for coming."

The meeting broke up. Turner still stood at the front of the room, his eyes locked onto Honey probingly.

"Emotions run high on this issue," Gerry said and sighed. "How long do you think it will take to do this investigation of yours?"

Turner's expression was still taut and angry, though the emotions were not as evident on his face as on Honey's. "That will depend on the number of mines involved and the size of the area to be covered. I'll want photos taken and timber samples of each mine in question. It depends on who I get to help me do the work." He fingered his chin in thought. "Perhaps two weeks, maybe as much as a month."

Gerry glanced at a mutinous Honey, throwing her a warning look that clearly told her to behave herself. "I can assure you that our Vice-Commander is the best and most reliable, not to mention the most available person for the job. She knows where most of the mines are located. There are no maps to follow on your own. In addition, most of our members have jobs that would prevent them taking two weeks or certainly a month off. But Honey owns, through her husband's estate, a fairly good-sized and profitable ranch on the edge of town. She has a competent manager to handle the business and I know she's been interested in this mine problem for a long while. She could be invaluable to you."

"She could be, but she won't be," Turner said. "I doubt she has the emotional control to deal impartially with this subject and I don't have the time to sort out the fact from the fantasy with her. I need the cold, hard facts; unfeeling as that may sound to both her and you. She can't give me that. I won't work with her; I'll have to find someone else."

"You're probably right." Honey circled the remaining chairs to come face to face with him, preventing Gerry from defending her further with a wave of her hand. "Someone else *will* have to do. But you won't find someone that cold or inhuman or unfeeling in this town . . . or anywhere else. You're one of a kind, Mr. Jameson. They broke the mold when they made you. You want someone without compassion, like yourself. I agree with you. It won't be me!"

CHAPTER TWO

HONEY SIPPED HER iced tea absentmindedly and set the glass down, swirling the ice chips and sliver of lemon around and around with her spoon to give her preoccupied fingers something to do.

"Do you want anything else, Honey? Is everything all right?"

"No thank you. The tea's fine." She took the check from her waitress, ignoring the curious glance and the double meaning of her last question. She didn't feel like talking about it when actually there was nothing to say. Turner Jameson was not going to help her; it was as simple as that, and yet not as simple. Even she knew the hurt she felt was all out of proportion. She had certainly read more into his letters than he had, in reality, promised. She had expected some knight in shining armor and she had gotten a man who looked like every girl's dream of prince charming, but was more of a dragon, breathing fire against her. So what was she really disappointed about? That he had not necessarily come to help the

Search & Rescue group as a whole, or that he had not come to help her? That he had not come to fill the gaping holes in the desert which were such a danger to the people around them, or that he had not come to fill the gaping holes in her life that Daryl had left when he died?

The bell on the door of the little café jingled warningly and Honey sank down deeper into the corner booth hoping to remain anonymous for the time being, at least until she figured out just how she was supposed to feel and just what she could do about it.

"You can't stay here forever, Honey Caldwell. You've got to go home sometime." Teresa scooted into the opposite side of the booth with a glass of beer clutched in one hand and a pizza tin and plates precariously balanced on the other.

"Here, have a piece. You missed Gerry's chili." She lobbed a partially congealed mass onto one of the plates and slid it in front of Honey.

"I'm not going to eat that." Honey occasionally wondered at her friend's sensitivity.

"Then what are you doing in a café? Why aren't you home?"

Honey's eyes flashed a warning. She was in no mood to be questioned. After Daryl died, Teresa had been the only one able to coax her back into the world of the living, bullying her into eating, dressing, and going about her daily business, exorcising the ghosts that haunted her by talking about them unceasingly in her matter-of-fact way until the pain faded to bearable levels. This was different though, and she wasn't ready to deal with it unemotionally. She changed the subject.

"Didn't you have any of Gerry's chili either?"

"Umhumm," Teresa mumbled through a large mouthful of pizza. "But that was *hours* ago, before we turned Pahrump topsy-turvy looking for you. Where *have* you been. And don't tell me here! We looked here and everywhere else in town at least twice."

Honey pushed a wave of sunburnt gold hair back. "I drove around. Just around, and if you must know, I didn't go home because I assumed Turner would be taken there. I mean, he *is* living there now. I should have taken him myself, introduced him to Pauline . . ." She paused in self-recrimination. "But I just couldn't."

"He's there. I took him myself," Teresa said. "But I didn't have to introduce him to Pauline. She already knew him, remember? He was Daryl's friend, after all."

"With friends like him, Daryl didn't need any enemies! And, I had forgotten. Of course Pauline would know him, it's just that I have a hard time picturing him here in town, living the kind of life that we do. He's so different from what I thought he would be . . . so very different from Daryl." An expression of wistful sadness and disappointment slipped through.

"He isn't Daryl, Honey, but you can't hold that against him," Teresa said softly. "Look, I don't know how you came to believe he had offered his help, but I've spent the last couple of hours with him, talking about you and the situation, looking for you, and I do know that what you expected and what he offered were two different things. Still, he hasn't said he won't help us, only that he wants proof," she admitted somewhat skeptically. "And he's been trying to recruit someone here in the valley to help him find it."

"I wish him luck," Honey snapped maliciously.

"That's just the point. Without you he'll have no luck, he'll have no proof, and everything you've worked for, everything *we've* fought to accomplish, will be thrown out the window. You're giving up without a fight, and that's not like you. Just talk to him. He's outside right now and I've convinced him to at least listen to your side of the story . . ."

"I thought he was at the house!" Honey stood, aghast, almost spilling the remainder of her unfinished tea in the process. She recovered and rummaged in her purse for change to pay the bill.

"Et tu, Teresa? Thanks! I'll tell you what I *know*. I know that Daryl could not have chosen a more disloyal friend. I know this town could not have a more unfaithful champion. I know that your Mr. Jameson has not lived up to my expectations. And I know I don't want to talk to him about it!" She held up a hand to ward off Teresa's defence of him. "And I'll tell you one thing more—if I hadn't promised to allow him to live under my own roof, I'd make it a point never to see him again. As it is—"

"As it is, you're going to have to see me, whether you like it or not," Turner said sharply and Honey whirled. "And I won't have you blaming Teresa for bringing me here. With or without her help, I would have found you: Pahrump is hardly big enough for you to hide in for long."

The air in the little café practically sizzled with electricity and a hush fell over the other diners as Turner spoke, his comments loud and rasping, his stance defiant, with hands on hips and legs set far apart, effectively blocking her intended avenue of escape.

When had he come in and how much had he heard? Worse, how much had he surmised? Honey held herself proudly erect.

"I don't want to see you," she hissed.

He growled at her, his irritation finding a focal point. "Then close your eyes, lady, but open your ears, and, if it's possible, your mind, because I need to get a few things straight with you!"

The anger burned hot in her veins, and once released, it refused to be contained under the cool, emotionless mask she wore in public. "Don't you think you've said quite enough for one day? Do you know how I felt hearing you suggest at the meeting that Daryl could have been responsible for his accident and perhaps the death of the person he tried to rescue? That even though you have the power and authority to perhaps close the mines, you might not exercise your option to do so? I told everyone that you were once his *friend!*" She spat the words at him like an accusation. "Friend? My God, how you can make that claim now and live with your conscience I'll never know. No! You're an outsider now and you've just abdicated any rights to command my attention."

She tried to sweep past him, but found herself jerked into his hold before she could pass, his fingers biting deeply into the flesh of her upper arms. He held her in an embrace so close one could have assumed them to be lovers were it not for the glint of anger, still unquenched in their eyes.

"Let go of me!" she demanded. "What kind of a cold, unfeeling man are you? If you had cared about Daryl, you wouldn't be here demanding we deliver some tangible proof for you to see and show off to your VIP associates, you'd be out there looking for it yourself. No, if you cared half as much as I do, you'd be manufacturing it! But then, if you had really cared about Daryl or his family, you would have been here eighteen months ago when the accident happened, not now as a means to assuage your guilt before you write mine safety legislation right out of your budget as unnecessary!"

The color drained from his face and his hold on her tightened. She couldn't remember ever seeing anyone as angry.

"Viper tongued little snake!" he whispered for her ears alone. "If you would only try to listen to my explanations."

"I don't want to hear any of your explanations!" she cried.

"The rest of the restaurant probably *does*, but unless you want them to, you'd better quiet it down." Teresa entered her observation pointedly. "Why don't you two have it out somewhere else, like home?"

"Not there." Turner barked, directing his criticism to Honey. "Since the meeting adjourned, your friends, which from the looks of things, number half the town, have been dribbling in over there in twos and threes to find out if you're okay and to crucify me. From their point of view, I came down too hard on you and have probably permanently injured your tender psyche. I don't know what they would have done to me if Teresa hadn't suggested we go look for you." He folded his arms and stood aloof from her. The only indication that his anger had not abated was a tightening around his mouth and eyes that had turned opaque and unreadable. "Speaking from purely selfish reasons, I wish you'd reassure them that you are more than able to defend yourself before they take matters into their own hands and run me out of town on a rail."

She hesitated. "I really don't want to see them right now." She had kept her feelings in check when Daryl died and after, never giving way to the anguish she felt in public, and seldom in private. She'd clung to the hope that if she could have some sort of revenge against the abandoned mines, if she could see them closed, then some of the hurt and frustration would vanish, then the whole terrible time in her life could be put to rest. To hear her hopes dashed had been a shock she could not conceal. It was no wonder her friends were worried. Yet she hadn't decided where to go from here and she couldn't face them until she knew . . . something.

"I don't see why not." Turner broke into her thoughts. "You look like tragedy personified, and if it's public support you're after, a performance like that should have your tiny post office overloaded with mail from irate citizens to your senators and congressmen. You'll get your mines closed all right, but it won't be through me."

"Do you mean you won't live up to your promise to investigate?" Teresa asked.

Turner stared at Honey unblinking, placing the blame on her shoulders. "How can I? I don't know where the mines are and I think Mrs. Caldwell's managed to make pretty damn sure no one's going to show me, that is, unless she decides to stop behaving like a spoiled child and show me herself."

"I thought I was unacceptable to you," Honey returned haughtily.

"You've left me with no other choice, lady. So, do we talk?"

"It can't hurt to talk," Teresa said.

Honey debated her position. It would be common

knowledge by morning, that they had fought, dramatized
in one-act scenes in gossipy coffee shop groups all over
town.

"I'll go. Let's get out of here."

She could feel the curious eyes on her hot face as they
walked the length of the café, past the slot machines that
were going full tilt this time of the late afternoon, their
patrons gratefully absorbed in the winning and losing of
money and not on her, past the open doorway that led
from the eating section of the restaurant to the bar.

"Thass a way to treat yer women... Gotta lettem
know who's the boss."

Honey ignored the slurred-voiced remark and slid
through the door to the outside. She didn't look back,
knowing he still followed from the crunch of gravel behind her, until she reached the parking lot and the Bronco
she'd left there. She hopped up onto the car's hood,
perched there, her chin cupped between her hands, waiting. The silence between them was uncomfortable, but
she was determined not to be the one to break it. She
watched him instead, the adrenaline still coursing through
her body sharpening her senses to him, to the spicy musk
of his aftershave, to the almost physical contact of his
body standing so close to her own. And despite herself,
the anger she had kept banked, ready to flare into life
again began to make a subtle metamorphosis, still as
intense, but with a different meaning. She looked away,
disgusted with herself. What kind of a woman was she
to respond to a man's animal attraction when she couldn't
stand him personally? "So where do we go? Or do we
talk here?"

"I'll let you know when we get there." He tossed the
keys to his Mercedes to a cautious Teresa who had come
from the café. "Try to keep the knights at bay for a while,
will you Teresa?" He captured Honey's hand and winced
as her fingernails dug into the flesh of his palm. Still he
held tight as he walked with her, then shoved her into
the passenger's side of her own Bronco. "Tell them they
can throw me to the lions if there's anything left after

this she-cat gets finished," he shouted to Teresa.

He started the generally cantankerous engine without trouble and left Teresa far behind.

"Don't you ever ask before you take possession of things that don't belong to you?"

"Never," he said definitely. "At least not if I'm sure permission would be denied. It saves on arguments that way." He added as an afterthought, "usually."

He followed the main street out of town as though he knew where he was going, veering finally off the highway and onto a dirt track that led up into the mountains. The cracked and pitted road led up from the searing heat of the desert floor and toward the high hills. They were covered with sage and hardy pine that clung to life in the sand that made up the soil even that high up and further still. Where were they going? No one lived this far out of the town in this particular direction that she knew of, unless it was the odd gold miner or hermit, certainly no one that a man like Turner would have any connection with.

"Figured it out yet or shall I tell you?"

He read her thoughts with a startling accuracy, more amazing because they had driven for some time in silence, broken only by the sound of the wind and of the brush as it scraped the sides of the Bronco in passing. It bothered her that he seemed to have little difficulty in reading her mind. She hadn't come to terms with how she felt about him herself yet and she didn't like the intimacy of him knowing her feelings before she did.

"It doesn't matter. One place is as good as another, and we won't be here long. It won't take long to say whatever we have to say to each other."

"I wouldn't be too sure of that if I were you."

She didn't delve into the meaning of that enigmatic response. Instead she concentrated on the terrain ahead as the road narrowed, spiraling up and coiling around itself, the encroaching brush all but obliterating the twisting pathway.

"It's deteriorated; but then fifteen years makes a difference in everything."

The information, such as it was, was not directed to her but to himself as he drove, his course necessarily slow but unfaltering. The roadway may have altered in appearance, but the route was the same for he knew where he was going. Coming to an abrupt stop, he climbed from the driver's seat. He parted the brush in front of the vehicle to reveal a barbed-wire fence and a rusted padlock on an even rustier gate that barred their way. It was so overgrown with the desert foliage that had Honey been driving, they would have crashed head on into it.

"Which way now?" She joined him at the gate and watched as he inserted a key partway into the rusted lock.

"Damn," he muttered. "Not through here for sure. I hadn't counted on this, though I suppose I should have." Taking the driver's seat again he followed the fence along for a few hundred feet until he came to a tear large enough to drive the Bronco through, then did so, careful of the sharp stones and wire barbs that were strewn along the edge. The trail worsened at that point until finally it was no more. They faced a lonely adobe structure, its paint faded and peeling, its plaster covering cracked in places, revealing the earth and straw construction underneath. If it was a home, the sounds of laughter had been missing from within for a very long time.

"Who does it belong to?" The interested question slipped out.

"Me," he said. "It was left to me, or rather to the idealistic boy I was when I left here. I had great plans for it once. My stepfather lived here until he died a few months back."

"I'm sorry." The words were polite, nothing more. She didn't want to feel genuine sorrow, she didn't want to feel anything for this man who seemed so unmoved by her own loss, who seemed so callous.

"We weren't close." He shrugged her expression of sympathy aside. "Hence the locked gate. He's partly the reason I left here fifteen years ago, though, as it turns out, I should thank him. If not for him, I'd still be here trying to earn a bare subsistence living farming this poor excuse for soil, and wondering if I had what it took to make it in the real world."

She took a deep breath of the clear mountain air, interrupting his brooding silence. "The real world, did you say? If this isn't real, what is? Not your crowded boardrooms where statistics and rules and regulations take precedence over people." She looked out over the rocks, leaving him to think that one over. From their rocky vantage point it was possible to get an aerial view of the valley below, crisscrossed with a patchwork of varying greens and browns, alfalfa and cotton interlaced with strips of dry desert sand and sage until the flatlands met the mountains, tinged now with the dusky purple of late afternoon and early evening. A picture postcard view set against an azure sky backdrop. Wasn't any of this real to him?

"There are times that it doesn't seem real. In the city there's very little time to contemplate where one's been or even where one is now. Your thoughts are always on tomorrow. Pahrump is very different from that, always has been, almost as if it's been caught in time. It doesn't change, not in atmosphere, as if it exists in a world by itself, and a world that I don't know how to belong to any more." There was something about the way he spoke that made her sure he wished, at times, that he could belong. Aware of her scrutiny he turned from the panorama and followed the overgrown trail that led to the back of the house, stepping around the encroaching bushes that threatened to engulf the small dwelling.

She followed, stopping with him as he knelt beside a roughly cemented irregularly shaped hole in the ground, half filled with crystal cool water.

"A swimming pool?" she ventured.

"And you call me an outsider," he mocked her lightly. "The stream that supplies the house with water dries up every summer and this . . . reservoir has to supply what water is needed until the rains come. Though you weren't all that wrong. Many's the time Daryl and I used it as a pool in the summer."

She stiffened perceptibly.

"You don't like to discuss him with me, do you?"

"Not now," she admitted. "You wanted to explain something to me?" Best to get down to the business at hand and stay away from any personal conversation.

"You won't make this easy for me, will you?" He studied her unrelenting expression. "Daryl and I grew up together, went to college together, and, contrary to what you choose to believe, were very much alike. The main difference was that he chose to come back to Pahrump and raise alfalfa and hopefully a bunch of kids, and, as much as I wanted to do the same thing, I had no huge ranch to come back to. All I had was this..." He waved a disparaging hand around him. "... and a strong desire to succeed where my own father had failed. Even so, I might have come home lots of times if my stepfather hadn't have been here. As it was, I couldn't come home, I had to succeed where I was, and I did. My job took me around the country, and though Daryl and I kept in touch over the years, I never came back, until now." His voice fell. "My mail tends to follow me around all over the country like a bedraggled bird's tail with bits and pieces of it falling off, never to be seen again. I never knew about Daryl's death, though Pauline assures me that a letter was sent. I didn't know until your letter came across my desk."

She began to fit the pieces together. "So when your letter came, offering to help, and to conduct an investigation, you didn't mean helping by closing the mines, you hadn't received any of our other letters?"

"No. My offer of help referred to...to...arrangements or perhaps a bit of business advice about the ranch until you could get things sorted out. I had no idea Daryl had been gone for eighteen months. My offer to have the mines investigated was just that, not a promise to close them up. I've violated my own personal conflict-of-interest rule by coming here myself as it is. When I realized you had all but published it in the newspaper that I was going to use my influence to help your cause, I admit to feeling used." He sighed. "You have no idea how many women have tried to use their personal influence and friendship with me. Many have tried to use the fact I'm attracted to them as a lever, as a means to lobby, if you will, for whatever cause they think I might be able to help with."

"But I couldn't be doing that." Honey shook her head in consternation. "For one thing, I had never met you. For another..." She laughed. "You don't strike me as the kind of man to succumb to persuasion. I think that the only thing that would convince you about the dangers of our mines is if I allowed you to go searching for them alone and you, excuse the pun, stumbled onto, or into, one of them yourself."

"I think you underestimate your own powers of persuasion," he answered her softly, allowing her to see the emotions that played on his face. "Don't pretend you don't know what I mean. Besides the fact that you're Daryl's wife, and I might be inclined to let things sway your way concerning the mines because of that, you're an incredibly beautiful woman, a little like a wild desert flower, and I've been attracted to you since Daryl sent me a picture of you on your wedding day." He took his wallet from his pocket and removed a photo of her and Daryl. "The difference now is that there is no person or distance to prevent my interest. The problem is that I make it a point never to mix business with pleasure, never to let emotional involvements interfere with my business decisions. I need you along with me on this investigation, though. So what to do?"

She flushed a deep scarlet and quickly lowered her eyes to the ground. "I don't know what to say. Daryl is gone, but I still consider myself married. I wouldn't consider having a relationship with you..." Liar, she told herself. "And I surely wouldn't consider using any relationship I did have to sway your decisions."

"I'm glad to hear it, because I've come to a decision about you coming with me on this investigation. Now hear me out. You need me if you ever hope to have a

chance to close the mines. I need you to help conduct
a thorough investigation."

"You can't ask me to be objective," she said quickly.

"Then you'd better hope I can be objective enough
for the both of us."

She had meant she couldn't be objective about the
mines, that she would do anything . . . she corrected herself . . . almost anything to see them closed. She had a
feeling he was referring to something else entirely.

"So . . . you're taking me with you?"

Whatever private war he had waged with himself over
the conflict of interest, there was no sign of it in his
definitive answer. "Yes, I'm taking you."

Like a hawk staking out territory.

She quelled the elation that welled up inside her at
the thought. She would be spending the next few weeks
with him for Daryl's sake . . . Daryl's! Not for herself.
What she had told him was true; she was married to
Daryl in spirit and Turner Jameson could mean nothing
to her. She held on to that thought and planted her feet
firmly on the ground, where she wanted them to stay for
the duration of his visit.

CHAPTER THREE

THE SKY HAD barely begun to color itself a pale pastel yellow on the horizon when Honey awoke, yet the room was warm already, even at predawn, promising another scorcher of a day. Flicking the sheet off, she rolled over in the wide double bed and tried to will herself back to sleep. It was too early to face the day, yet all the problems and questions that had filled her mind the day before and interrupted her usually dreamless sleep crowded in again, refusing to be banished.

"Five fifteen?" She rubbed her eyes and mumbled the question to the digital clock on her nightstand as it blinked the time sluggishly. This would never do. She had the feeling she'd need all her wits about her today and in the days to come, and this morning she felt about as unprepared for battle as it was possible to be.

She padded into the hallway toward the kitchen in search of some instant fortification, rummaging through the cupboards for powdered milk, sugar, and freeze-dried coffee, while waiting for the water to boil.

"Ssssshhhhh," she admonished the inanimate pan illogically as the water bubbled over, extinguishing the flame with a hiss. Just because she couldn't sleep was no good reason to wake the rest of the household.

"Is this a private party, or can anyone join?"

The fire-hot liquid sloshed over the mug and onto her hand, and she gasped audibly, dropping the cup, fortification and all on the floor.

"Turner! What in heaven's name are you doing in here?" She held the scalded hand to her lips, frozen where she stood, and compared her own sleep-tossled appearance with his. Wasn't he ever mussed? The rich brown hair was damp, as if recently washed, but there wasn't a curl out of place and his clothes, though relatively casual compared to yesterday's attire, still had that crisp pressed look. Even his shoes were shined.

"Did you burn yourself?"

"Very observant!" She tossed him a withering look. "A little. You startled me. What are you doing up at this time of morning?"

"I'm an uprooted farm boy remember? It's a habit I've never gotten away from."

She turned the sink taps to cold and put her afflicted hand under the spray. Why? What do you do at five A.M. in an apartment? Prune your house plants?"

He lifted an eyebrow. "I watch the sunrise."

"Through the smog I imagine." She wasn't feeling any too agreeable. Her hand still hurt every time she lifted it from the cooling water, and she wasn't used to conversing with strange men in her kitchen. She looked for a hand towel, and not finding one, flicked droplets of water on the floor uneasily.

"I'll . . . I'll be right back."

Sitting once again on the edge of her bed, she was inspecting the burn in privacy until the door swung open and Turner reappeared, a tube of ointment in one hand and another cup of coffee in the other.

"Here, let me see that." He took her hand before she could stop him and began rubbing the salve there.

"You must be one of those people who isn't civil until they've had their first cup of coffee in the morning. Here, drink up. You need it."

She took it from him, deciding to drink it rather than obey her first impulse which was to douse him with it, and allowed him to finish spreading the salve, his fingers sending comforting messages racing along her nervous system.

"Thank you," she relented finally—and only coincidentally after all of the coffee in the cup was gone. "I suppose I did snap your head off."

"It's no wonder." He left her alone to open the heavy brocade drapes a little wider, flooding the room with sunlight. "Much better," he said to himself.

"What is?" She watched curiously as he circled the room slowly, picking up and discarding various objects at random, Daryl's competition pistols, the ribbons, the trophies he'd won at various meets, the picture she kept of him beside the bed.

"I said it's no wonder you're irritable and depressed in the morning. If I had to sleep in a mausoleum every night, I probably wouldn't keep my sunny nature either."

Honey opened her mouth to defend the room, then closed it again. She *had* felt that it was a little like sleeping in a shrine, but she'd never told anyone. "I don't spend much time here."

"I shouldn't wonder." He turned to her in amazement. "You know, this place has hardly changed since I used to visit as a boy?"

She didn't know whether he was censuring her or merely reminiscing.

"We planned to build our own home, Daryl and I," she explained. "And there didn't seem to be any sense in redecorating here, when we wouldn't be here long. Later . . . afterwards . . . Pauline couldn't bear to see anything changed." She paced the confines of the room with him, taking a fresh look at her surroundings, the furnishings, all reminders of Daryl and the life they had shared together. "Her mental condition was and is very fragile. I think she wanted to believe that if everything was the same, then he wouldn't really be gone. And it does seem as if he'd just left for a moment, that he's coming back..."

Turner didn't respond at all, studying her with an uncomfortably direct attention.

"Well, and this room isn't the only thing. She's never sold his favorite riding horse, and sometimes she lays an extra place at the table during the holidays, fixes his favorite foods... I'm sure you understand."

If she hoped to find approval from him, she was wrong. "I understand all too well," he agreed softly, but there was a dark anger hidden just under the surface of his placid words. "I imagine his clothes are still hanging in the closets." He threw open her wardrobe doors to prove the point.

"You have no right..." She shut them again, barring his way with her body.

"And to complete the picture, she has you here, where she plans to keep you as a... a sort of living reminder. Be thankful you weren't pregnant or she'd never allow you to leave. I thought burying wives alive with their dead husbands went out with Egyptian pharaohs. But here you are..." He reached out to touch the filmy pale gold robe she wore over a nightgown of the same material, a present from Pauline on her last birthday. "Here you are, dressed like this. You could be a bride awaiting your husband... a woman in love, waiting for her lover to come."

"I didn't ask you here to approve of my nightclothes or my bedroom." She snatched the material from his fingers. "Come to think of it, I didn't ask you to come in here at all. You came uninvited."

He didn't raise his voice to match hers, keeping his low so that she had to be quiet to hear what he had to say. "Don't misunderstand me, Honey. I didn't say there was anything wrong with what you're wearing. And I think the bedroom is the perfect place to display your... charms. I heartily approve of this frothy little bit of nothing, at least I would if it were worn to entice me . . . or any living, breathing, flesh and blood man. But the man you bought it to please, the man you're wearing it to tempt is beyond temptation. He's been dust for eighteen months, and to think about him in any kind of a physical sense is going to be nothing more than frustrating and it won't do you a damned bit of good."

She felt her muscles contract, felt the sting of her palm as her hand met his cheek, but he continued on undaunted, the imprint of her hand red and dark against his skin.

"Pauline isn't the only Caldwell who needs convincing that Daryl isn't going to come back, is she?" he demanded. "That's what you're really upset about, isn't it? You've spent the past year and a half trying to close the mines, *not* for safety's sake, but as a monument to him. And I was fine, I was welcome as long as you could see me as Daryl's loyal friend and you could see me helping you achieve that goal. But you can't see me that way because I don't fit that image; you see me as a man . . ."

"No!"

"You may not like it, but it's true. And I sure don't think of you as Daryl's poor grieving widow. I see you as a woman, with needs and wants beyond what this room has to offer you, and you don't know how to react to that."

"That's crazy. I don't have those kinds of feelings anymore."

"That's crazy. And I don't believe it for an instant. But if *you* still do, then I'm here to change your mind because I do have those feelings and I've had them for you since I first saw your picture." He tangled his fingers in a heavy stand of her hair. "If you're right, then what I'm about to do won't affect you at all, but it's going to do me a world of good."

Before she could move or speak he had covered the small distance between them and was pushing her against the closet door, holding her there with his body. He lightly claimed her lips with his, testing her, tasting her like a fine wine not to be had often and only at a great price, molding the contours of her mouth to his ever so lightly in a contact that nonetheless hit her senses like a ton of bricks. She found that she did not, could not object when his tongue caressed the inside of her mouth, searchingly tender. She moaned softly, acknowledging that in the flesh, at least, he had been right. She wanted him . . . a little, maybe more than a little, and she allowed him to pull her still closer until she could feel his very flesh and muscles strain to complete the contact. Her lips had that full, red-tinged, well-kissed look when he released her suddenly.

"Do you still feel that the desire I spoke of having for you is a one-way street?" He mouthed the query almost silently so as not to break the spell of the moment.

She shook her tawny gold hair negatively and gazed up at him with eyes that had stopped doubting what he had to tell her.

He took advantage of the vulnerable moment to let his eyes wander lower, to those areas not kissed by the burning sun, to be seen through the silky, translucent negligee. He pushed the robe off one shoulder to further reveal the creamy swell of her breasts, their rose-tipped nipples taut and clearly defined under the diaphanous fabric.

"You're rather like a prickly pear, do you know that? With prickly defensive spines on the outside, ready to wound anyone who dares to come too close. But once through the barrier, you're a sweet and utterly delicious cactus fruit." He lowered his head to nibble kisses and soft, half-intelligible words into her neck, but she moved too fast, finding her legs and her strength of will at last.

"Get out." She held the door open for him, fighting to hide the humiliation she felt was visible all over her. She did not look into the hall, did not see anyone there until a mocking voice made her aware.

"Don't tell me *you* are mixing business with pleasure, Turner? Or is it pleasure you're mixing with business?"

The woman who stepped half into the room was every

bit as sophisticated as her voice had sounded, from her high-heel dress shoes to the top of her artfully colored short ash-blond hair. Fashionably thin, her sleek frame looked business-like in a navy blue blazer and skirt, only the ruffled blouse underneath, the same shade as her bright red lipstick, hinting at a desire to appear feminine. Yet, as she walked toward Turner, her every movement was calculated to attract.

"Charlene?" Turner seemed surprised. "My business associate." He explained quickly to Honey.

Some business associate, she thought, unless they had the same business/pleasure arrangement the woman had accused her of having with him. The woman draped herself around him, a Siamese cat bent on getting full attention with her throaty purr.

"Well, aren't you going to introduce us? Aren't you going to ask why I'm here?"

"I did wonder why you were so far afield." Turner was once more in control, his question indulgently amused. Honey was forgotten for the time being, left unceremoniously to gather her wits.

"When you called yesterday to say your promise of help on this assignment had been reniged upon by the local yokels, I was called upstairs. We decided that since we've worked so well together before, I should lend a hand. Now, that is . . ." She looked down her nose at Honey, "unless you've managed to charm your way out of the little difficulties you spoke of—which I gather you haven't."

Honey bristled at the term yokels. She'd already decided she didn't much like the woman, and that hadn't helped. Nevertheless she extended a hand which was reluctantly and limply accepted.

"I'm Honey Caldwell. I'm going to be guiding Mr. Jameson around to allow him to investigate the mines. You *did* catch us having a difference of opinion, but not a change in plan. It was a simple misunderstanding."

"Mmmm." Charlene nodded unconvinced. "Well you haven't cornered the market on misunderstandings." Her

eyes flew back to Turner. "You wouldn't believe the
trouble I had getting here. All we had to go by at the
office was an address, no directions. Then to come here!
What is this place, Pahrump? A speck on the map, with
no streetlights or street signs and nothing open." She
shuddered as if the effort had been horrendous. "When
I finally stumbled on this house . . . purely by accident
mind you . . . I thought it *must be* the motel you were
staying at; I mean everyone else lives in tin trailers . . ."

"Mobile homes," Honey corrected. And there were
many regularly constructed homes here now, too, though
Charlene did have a point about street signs.

"Whatever," she continued. "At any rate, it took me
fifteen minutes to wake this poor woman and make her
understand that I was with you and that I simply *had* to
have a room for the night. Well, of course she offered
me one, and it was only as I was unpacking that I dis-
covered this was a private home. By that time the poor
creature must have thought me mad and gone off to bed.
I can tell you, I'm exhausted. I do hope you appreciate
this."

He groaned in sympathy with her. "I do. Now look,
why don't you take the morning to catch up on your
beauty sleep. Mrs. Caldwell and I can look after the
details until this afternoon."

"Mrs. Caldwell?" Charlene frowned. "You must be
related to the fair-haired woman who let me in last night."

"That's right. She's my mother-in-law," Honey said.

"Mother-in-law?" Charlene glanced around the room.
"And your husband is . . . out of town?"

"Rather permanently, I'm sorry to say Charlene."
Turner came to her rescue dryly. "Now why don't you
go back to bed and get up on the right side this time."

She pouted at him prettily. "Good thought. But,
Turner, we can't stay here and impose on the Caldwells.
Why don't we just go and look for commercial lodgings
in . . . town, if that's possible, unless you think you could
manage to gloss over this investigation and get us back
somewhere a little more civilized by nightfall?"

Now there's an idea. Honey waited hopefully. He could just agree to close the mines and save them all what was shaping up to be one heck of a lot of trouble.

"I can't do that."

From the look on Charlene's crestfallen face, he'd not only dashed Honey's hopes but hers as well.

"I've got to investigate all the mines and that's going to take weeks, even considering the help I've been promised. I can't rule either way without some hands-on observations. So . . ." He came back to Honey. "Can you possibly manage to put us both up here?"

Barely. "You're both welcome to stay as long as necessary." She extended the invitation with as much polite warmth as she could manage without choking on the words. What else could she do?

"We'll see that you and your mother-in-law are adequately reimbursed," Charlene offered.

"Mr. Jameson was my late husband's friend," Honey refused the offer coldly. "One has obligations to one's friends. He would want me to offer his hospitality." Get that message, Turner Jameson? She held the door wider for him to leave, but only Charlene stepped back out into the hall.

"Thanks. I think I'd rather stay here than brave the roads again anyway. Call out if you need me, otherwise I'll see you both this afternoon, after I've recovered."

Honey looked to Turner to see if he would follow, but he did not, remaining stationary.

"Are you hinting that you'd like me to leave you in peace?" He had known well she wanted him gone.

Peace? She had known no peace since laying eyes on him, wasn't even sure she knew what that state of mind was anymore. All she knew for sure was that, to use his analogy, he had stripped her of her prickly pear defenses so thoroughly that she had almost betrayed Daryl's memory in his arms, had laid her secrets bare for him to see, for all to see. And Charlene Mercer looked tough enough to eat nails for breakfast. She'd surely have no trouble digesting prickly pear spines, if even that defense was left to her. She passed a hand over her face, subconsciously trying to wipe away the guilt she felt was written there, for actions she could not defend. How had her life become so complicated so quickly?

"I just want you to leave." She sighed, wishing that when he did she could crawl back into bed as Charlene had done. She dismissed that thought; no rest for the wicked. "I'm going to get dressed and call Teresa, see about those volunteers in need. I imagine you'll want to get right to work."

"So that I can be done with it and get out of your life?" He handed her the robe, draping it modestly across her shoulders. "Your defenses, prickly pear."

CHAPTER FOUR

THEY WORKED LIKE demons were among them for the rest of the morning, Honey and Gerry and Teresa. And Honey wasn't so sure that a demon *wasn't* among them, embodied in the form of Turner Jameson who seemed to want to accomplish all that they had to accomplish in one day.

"Just who was it who signed me up for this slave labor camp? I couldn't have volunteered." Teresa tossed the question to her on the run, a hand full of year-old rescue reports that Turner had requested, under her arm.

"If I recall correctly, you volunteered yourself so that you'd be close at hand in case he ever got romantic ideas."

"Don't remind me." Teresa groaned her defeat. "The only ideas he's come up with so far involve more work. And speaking of work..." She stopped for a moment, resting the stack of reports on her hip. "Where is everybody when you need them? Don't tell me it's going to be just you and me and Gerry doing all this? Why is it that when we plan barbecues or fireworks *everybody*

41

finds time, but when we plan a work day all we get are excuses?"

Honey could only shrug. It was the way things went, a few volunteers doing all the work. She didn't want to think how much more difficult it would be if Turner didn't decide to close the mines and only a handful of members were actually left to police the entire park. "If it's any consolation to you, we aren't the only ones plagued with the problem. You think *we* have a cross to bear? You haven't met Turner's associate yet. She went upstairs early this morning to catch up on her beauty sleep. So far she's gotten enough to accommodate an entire pageant of lovelies...and if you want to know the truth, she didn't need much sleep to be a perfect '10' as it was."

"Meow," Teresa said, then laughed as she swept by. "I can hardly wait."

Honey sank down onto the living room couch, a list of "things-to-do" in her hand, grateful to be off her feet for a few minutes, even if it meant working at the same time. She checked off items they had finished.

"Review rescue reports," she read aloud. Turner had been at that all morning, taking over Pauline's kitchen table with the reports and his journal that grew ever larger. The man had a voracious appetite for facts... among other things. She dismissed that last thought with a frown and went down the list.

"Buy supplies: (a) food; (b) equipment. Well if we can charge it off to Turner's expense account, why not?" She added a few small items to her list, wishing she'd remembered them earlier. She'd already gone through a tank of gas running into Las Vegas for more freeze-dried food and various pieces of climbing equipment to supplement what the group had and various members offered to supply out of their own personal gear.

"Check first aid box." She made a mental list of what they had and what they might need, then scratched the figures out, rewriting newer, larger ones. With two inexperienced city people along, they'd undoubtedly need twice as much.

"Water and gas containers." She'd have to remember to check and see that they were all adequately filled and placed in the various vehicles to be taken, but that could be done last thing before they left tomorrow.

"Bring backpacks and sl . . ." She lifted her head at the voice.

"Honey!" An all too familiar command bellowed from the dining room. "I need you in here for a minute, please."

She sat spitefully immobile. Where was it written that he could commandeer her along with everything else for the duration?

"Honey!" More impatient this time.

"Coming!" She hollered in return, hoping her own inflections resembled a drill sergeant's as much as his did.

"He needs me for a minute . . . a minute my foot!" she grumbled in a normal tone of voice. "If I had a dollar for every minute I've given him today, I'd be a very rich woman."

"And if you had to pay me a dollar for every minute I've given you today, you'd be in debt up to your ears."

The doorbell rang before she could think of a comeback or to ask what was so important that he had left his command post to come look for her.

"To be continued," she cautioned him, "after we see who's here now." The volunteers had poured in all morning, offering equipment, mine locations, advice, etc., everything in fact that they could possibly need except for additional manpower. That commodity was not to be found. She crossed her fingers in hopes this caller would be different. She opened the door and stared at their visitor unblinkingly for a moment before whooping for joy and throwing herself into his arms. Her prayers were answered. Here was a volunteer made-to-order.

"Indian!" She hugged the older man tightly with affection and drew him into the room. "What brings you down from the mountain?"

"Rumors," he answered, looking beyond her to where Turner awaited.

"Oh, yes." She remembered her manners. "Turner, I'd like you to meet a very dear friend of mine. His real name is John, but everyone calls him Indian."

Turner looked at the old man, puzzled, wanting to fit the face in front of him with one from memory. Honey stood aside to give him a better view.

"And Indian, this is Turner Jameson. He's come from Reno, from the Bureau of Land Management. He's going to investigate the mines." She gave the introduction for Turner's benefit, not Indian's. If he was here, he already knew who Turner was and what he'd promised to do. Indian had an uncanny knack for turning up, a will-o'-the-wisp, knowing everything before anyone told him.

He was old, no one knew quite how old, including Indian himself, for he didn't have a birth certificate, but his parents had died over sixty years ago when he was just a small boy. Honey thought he certainly didn't look to be sixty-five plus. His long braided hair was gray, to be sure. And his piñon nut brown skin was weathered by time and the elements to a crinkled leathery texture, but there was a strength in abundance in his tall, and rather emaciated looking frame. She'd often thought he'd outlast them all. He had outlasted one of them...

"Here, don't let me keep you in the door. Come on in." She took his faded and well-patched denim jacket, noticing his pants were not as well kept, his shirt hem torn off to serve as a headband under the always worn battered leather cowboy hat. Still, for all that, he had a proud carriage that always reminded her of the great Indian chiefs he sometimes talked about. It was with a good measure of this dignity that he assessed Turner, and only after being sure that he liked what he saw, he held out a gnarled hand and clasped the younger man's in his own, both grips equally strong.

"You're not like the other city men I see come to the valley. You don't talk all the time. That's good."

He doesn't talk, just orders people around, Honey amended his observation silently.

"I've come to help you." He took the beer Honey

offered and spoke only to her.

"I'm grateful." She looked from one man to the other. *What* were they doing? "Indian knows this desert a thousand times better than I do, better than anyone else. If he's come to help, we don't need anyone else." Anything to make conversation.

"What can you show us? What can you tell me that will help?" It was Turner who broke the silence between them.

He was not answered directly. "You will not remember me, but I met you once, a long time ago when your father was still living, before that other one came. I know who you were; I know where your roots lie. What I can show you depends on how much you are willing to see. What I can tell you depends on how much you have forgotten and how willing you are to learn... and remember."

He touched the handcrafted silver and turquoise squash blossom necklace that he wore about his neck. In sharp contrast to his clothing, the necklace was valuable and very beautiful. Whatever subject he had hinted at before, the time for discussing it was over.

"About the mines you seek; I can show you quite a few, including the one this silver came from."

"Do you have rights to that mine?" Turner asked.

"In a manner of speaking. As much as any man with any sense can own a part of this desert. I used to take silver from it once in a while. I do not have one of your government claims for it, no."

Turner opened a map on the table to its fullest extent, circling in red broad tipped felt pen a large area of land, evidently unconcerned that the chunk of silver around Indian's neck had come from a mine he did not own. "The mines I am most interested in lie within these boundaries, within the boundaries of the park proposed—"

"I know of the park."

"Good. It saves time explaining." Turner wasn't allowing himself to be intimidated. "With Honey's help, and all that we've been offered today, I'm sure we can find several dozen of them."

"And I can show you many more that perhaps she does not know of."

"We can use your help. We don't have much time."

The conversation was interrupted as Charlene sauntered into the room, looking well rested and more refreshed than Honey thought anyone had a right to be at four P.M. in the afternoon.

"My! Aren't we busy as bees down here? Are you having trouble with the paperwork, Turner?" She touched a pile of papers and then another, not bothering to look at them. "What's happened to your usual efficiency?"

Teresa rolled her eyes heavenwards at Honey's disgusted expression, smiling sweetly at Charlene as the introductions were made. "I think we are more of a hindrance than a help, but then we aren't used to working with him, and no one else was available."

Bless you. Honey sent a silent "touché" to the "no one else" who had turned her attention back to Turner.

"And you haven't met Indian." He introduced the old man. "From everything I hear, he knows more about what we need to see than even Honey does. He's going to be a great asset to the project."

"Indian." Charlene had a pained expression on her face that read: quaint.

"Indian." Indian liked his nickname very much and repeated it for effect.

Charlene raised her delicately penciled brows and moved perceptibly away from him, wrinkling her nose at his unwashed looking appearance.

"I suppose if you're really that good, you can replace Mrs. Caldwell. I understand that she had to be persuaded to go and I know that her mother-in-law thinks she ought not to be involved in this mine thing at all, which is perfectly understandable, if you ask me."

Honey knew Pauline would prefer she not go anywhere near the mines, the very mention of them a painful reminder of all that she had lost. And as Turner had insinuated so nastily, she had often given in to her whims to keep the peace, but not in this. This time she had to follow her own instincts, and her instincts were telling her to go.

"I will be going," she said simply.

"But if you'd prefer not to..." Charlene lifted her shoulders as if to add that she would prefer it that way, too. "And in any case, we do have a limited budget, and if there are too many...helpers...or this thing drags on long, none of you will be making even minimum wage for your efforts."

Teresa snorted derisively. "As if we get paid a dime for all the work we do for Search & Rescue as it is. This is to help us, too."

Indian stood his ground, having allowed the windy woman to continue on unabated until she was finished. "I offer my help to Honey Caldwell at no cost that you would understand, but I would not work for the government for any price." He turned his back on Charlene deliberately and spoke to Turner. "I will be here tomorrow about sunrise. It will be best to get an early start before the sun is too hot."

"You know best."

Indian grunted at Turner's comment and waited for Honey to show him out. He picked up a sanded, somewhat crooked tree limb walking stick from where he'd left it just outside the door.

"Can I give you a ride somewhere?" Turner offered from the porch.

Indian lifted his moccasined feet and inspected the bottoms of them both. "These will take me as far as I need to go, further than your car could." He shook his head at the Mercedes parked out front as though it were an impossible vehicle. A lost cause. He looked back at Turner as if to question whether the man who drove it was too. "Pack the Bronco for tomorrow."

Perched crosslegged atop the hood of the Mercedes in the scalding sun at noon the next day, both she and the owner of that accursed city car wished that Turner had listened to Indian's advice. The day had not started well at all. Honey couldn't figure it out. She'd participated in any number of orchestrated rescues, organized in the heat of an emergency, on the spur of the moment, and she knew how well the group worked together under pressure . . . usually.

Today though was proof positive, so far, that Murphy's Law existed: If something can go wrong, it will, and it did for them, over and over again until she wondered if *Candid Camera* wasn't out there somewhere, hiding behind a clump of cactus filming the whole comedy of errors for posterity.

The Mercedes had been the first to go, its underbelly used to freeway travel and no match for what Turner termed the pest-ridden, pot-hole ridden, cactus-infested goat trail that led to the first mine.

Scratch one transport and two able-bodied workers.

The second stroke of nasty luck set the stage for the rest. An accident on the other side of town called one of their one-day-only volunteers, who also just happened to be on the ambulance crew, away to do a more important job. Unfortunately with directions and instructions being given all over the same emergency channel, the only one monitored with any regularity, the airways were, needless to say, crowded, resulting in people being scattered all over the valley.

At the moment, she and Turner were waiting for a tow truck to return from the scene of the accident where a dispatcher thought it was wanted.

"How long do you think it will take them to get here?"

Honey leaned back against the windshield in answer and settled herself in to wait. "How good are you at amusing yourself for an hour or so?"

"Not very." He drummed his fingers against his leg. "And that volunteer whats-his-name . . ."

"Bob."

"Bob has our gear?"

"Righto." She wasn't inclined for conversation. He

was the one who insisted they take the Mercedes to avoid any damage to private cars. She had *wanted* to take the Bronco; Gerry and Teresa had *insisted* on taking the Land Rover and the Jeep. She wished she'd been more assertive.

"Couldn't we call someone to fetch the gear and/or us?"

"I think we'd better stay off the air for a bit, don't you?" she responded dryly. "We're stuck here. Make the best of it."

"That's what I was afraid of." He sighed in frustration.

"Sorry." She tilted her head to one side, resting her cheek against the warm windshield glass.

"Me, too. We can't afford too many of these delays on our timetable. Still, there is a silver cloud."

"Hmmm?" She was ripe for good news.

"I've wanted to be alone with you for twenty-four hours now, and all I could do was watch you from afar, without touching you while everyone in Pahrump paraded in and out with more help. God, what a helpful town."

She couldn't tell if the fact amused or maddened him.

"I kept hoping that if I hurried, I could have you to myself for just a little while. Now I get the chance, and look at us."

She dropped her eyes uneasily and made a real effort to steer the talk back to more impersonal issues. "You did ask them to drop by if they could offer any help."

"So I did, and I appreciate it, but all I wanted yesterday was for them to go home and leave us alone."

"Wouldn't work; Pauline's there. It *is* her home. And then there's Charlene." She shifted her weight away from him without moving, hoping he wouldn't lean any closer.

"Charlene is a business associate, and I don't give a damn about what Pauline wants, and, in any case, neither of them matter now, because, due to my lack of foresight and our incredibly bad luck, we're here, and that's the silver cloud. It's just you and I."

"In the middle of the road, in the sun, on top of your car, with the tow truck coming at any minute."

"Honey," he said softly, "I seldom ask idle questions. You said yourself that the tow truck was on the far side of the valley and not likely at all to get here in under an hour. We have the time to talk undisturbed, no place to go, nothing else to do but wait." He rubbed his thumb across her chin. "Honey, look at me."

"Why?" She did not look up.

"Because I think you felt something when I held you yesterday, something you didn't expect to feel, something I only hoped you might someday. I don't know why it is this way between us, but I felt that pull from the first time I saw your picture, as I've told you. I think you're feeling it now."

She could keep the laughter or the tears inside, trapped there, held privately within for no one else to see, but her face had always been a giveway, expressive, portraying in moving art the emotions she was feeling, her eyes a window into which all could see.

The private quiet of the desert was a world into which she had often retreated, enjoying the stillness of a land as yet unpolluted by noise. Yet at this moment, she would have traded all that for the calliope of Las Vegas at night if it would have distracted Turner's intense concentration on her and her answer.

"I want to know if I have a chance with you. Pauline and Daryl and the mines and my past and yours aside, I want to know if you feel anything for me. If, as I believe, you do, we can build on that. I can make you forget all the rest. If you don't . . ." He looked as if he didn't want to consider that possibility. "I never waste time on impossibilities and lost causes." His eyes darkened with the same fierce determination that must have shown in their depths when he resolved to leave Pahrump. He had wanted another life for himself, perhaps a better life and he had gone after it. He was the master of his own destiny, with the ability to reshape events and even people to suit his own needs. He seemed very good at it, and he wanted her.

"I won't believe you feel nothing for me, Honey. You didn't reject me yesterday."

"I was surprised." She played for time. That much was true. She had been surprised. But then, Turner had been a continual source of surprise to her from the beginning.

"Then I hereby give you fair warning." He moved with an excruciatingly deliberate lack of speed, giving her time to move away if she could.

She could not.

She knew the touch of his lips could be stopped if she could find the right words, but she had no "right" words, her mouth refusing to cooperate with her mind's plea. Instead her lips opened slightly to receive the contact, a part of her drinking in the physical sensations, that same part responsible for shutting out the inevitable mental reservations. There was only Turner and she, she and Turner and the feeling she had been aware of . . . growing unbidden within her like the roadside wild flowers that grew in spite of the odds against them, coloring the otherwise drab desert around them. In the same way, Turner was a vivid splash of emotional color on the landscape of her life, a life that had been as barren as a moonscape for so long.

And she was not passive in his arms. Once the first move had been made, and by him, her body responded in kind, becoming softer, more pliant under his touch. The distance between them lessened considerably, though she couldn't consciously recall moving toward him, the needs she felt giving her body a rhythm of its own, one that he was well attuned to.

He maneuvered his arms under her and around, pulling her closer, his hands massaging her bare back underneath the thin cotton shirt, his fingers clairvoyant, finding each sensitive nerve, sending shivers of forbidden delight coursing up and down her spine, forcing a moan from somewhere deep in her throat.

"Turner." She whispered his name feverishly.

"Yes, my love. Tell me! Tell me what you want from me."

She faltered, not wanting to put it into so many words. "I don't really know." She tried to close her eyes to the fact that she most certainly did know.

"You know as much as I do," he admonished her lightly. "And I can do and be everything you need." He caressed her shoulders for only a moment more. "But not here." He looked around as if he, too, had forgotten precisely where they were. "Not here in front of any person who might stumble by and for every ground squirrel to witness. Tell me again. Why are we sitting here, on top of the car in the sun, instead of in the shade in privacy?"

"In case they need to contact us for directions, the reception is better outside the car."

"Do we really want to give them a hand in finding us any time soon?"

A slight breeze cooled the space he had made between them, cooled too the passion that had threatened to run away with her.

"I've been confined in a city too long." He sighed regretfully upon seeing the look leave her face. "I should have taken you while I had the chance, while it was what we both wanted. I shouldn't have worried about Peeping Tom squirrels."

His attempt at humor failed.

"I wish this had never happened," she said in frustration. "I wish we could just go back to the beginning and be friends."

"We are friends. We'll be much more."

"I haven't said so." She took a comb from her pants pocket and ran it through her honey gold tresses that his hands had so recently tangled. Anything to avoid just sitting there vulnerable to his scrutiny and his questions.

"You haven't said so in so many words maybe, but it's true."

To continue to deny it might only provoke a further demonstration of his hold over her, but to remain silent would be an admission, a statement in itself. She was damned if she did and the same if she didn't. She took out the hand held radio instead and spoke into it, forcing normality into her speech.

"Break one nine, breaker nineteen, this is the Honey Bee..." She gave her handle over the radio. "I'm still waiting for a tow truck. Come on back, Tom, and let us know where you are."

The crackle grew louder as she adjusted the volume, then stilled as a deep male voice boomed over the airways. "Towin' Tom here, Honey Bee. Be with you shortly... Sorry for the delay. Over."

"He'll be here any time." She repeated the transmission unnecessarily, reminding him as well as herself that this time was no time for further madness.

"I'd be happy if the tow truck was my only obstacle." Turner repositioned the sun glasses on his nose. "Still, I don't mind working for what I want. I've worked hard for everything of value I've ever gotten. It makes victory all the sweeter."

"I'm not a prize to be won," she snapped.

"Oh, yes you are." The seductive quality had returned to his voice. "You're a prize I dreamed of having for a long time, but one that I never thought I'd have or have the opportunity to win. No, Honey, I have no intention of giving up on you without a battle."

She did not want to fight with him, having the distinct impression she might very well lose.

"The tow truck's here." And not a moment too soon. She watched the telltale cloud of dust in the distance and got off the hood of the Mercedes to wait for it long before it was necessary to do so.

"Have it your way," she heard him behind her. "I can be a patient man."

He said as much to the tow truck driver who predicted both a long wait at the local garage and more troubles of the same kind if the Mercedes was ever driven over similar ground again.

"You're going to have to invest in a good truck if you plan to stay around here long, Mister."

"Hmmmm," he agreed. "And a few other changes in my lifestyle, as well, I suspect."

CHAPTER FIVE

THE CHANGES IN lifestyle were quickly apparent when work began the next morning before the first light of dawn. It began with a cheery voice outside her door.

"Are you decent in there?" *He* who pounded on the door came in without waiting for her reply, mumbled half asleep, his hands loaded down with a number of oddly shaped aluminum foil bags. Leaving a trail of them from the door to the bed, he stood over her, raining packets of dehydrated scrambled eggs along with peas and carrots of the same variety down onto the coverlet.

"You have to help me," he ordered. "I don't know which ones to pack, and I'm packing now. Do we take the canned stuff or these? I saw both in the box you brought from Las Vegas the other day."

"Both," she mumbled sleepily. "Both if we were going camping, or backpacking, but coming back here as we are for meals, we really won't need either beyond emergency rations which we always carry."

"We'll need more."

She opened her eyes to peer questioningly at him. "Why?"

"Because I said so. Why do we need canned and dry?"

"Chauvinist answer," she snapped. "You need both because dehydrated is light and easy to pack, takes little space. It's good if you've the water to spare. The canned is better when you don't, though it's heavier. Besides, they don't dehydrate everything."

He inspected the bags closely. "If they can do ice cream, they can do anything."

She made a face. "It doesn't *taste* like ice cream. And I like Polish sausage. They don't dehydrate Polish sausage, or I don't think they do." She threw on a robe, a heavier variety than the one he had so admired the day before yesterday.

"And speaking of food, back to the original question; why do we need to take it with us?"

"Because I don't want to take the time to run back and forth from whatever mine site we're at to the house. I'll want to spend the entire day there, and if we run out of time, I may want to base all the operations from one of the vehicles and not come back in at all until we're finished with the investigation."

She raised an eyebrow. A change in lifestyle, indeed. How he'd fare without all the comforts of home that he had become used to in the past fifteen years might be something well worth seeing, but she didn't comment on that.

"If you'll give me a minute, I'll get dressed and make breakfast for all of us that are going from here . . . sort of a last supper and all that."

"You're too late. All of us who are going to be breakfasting here have done so. You can have yours on the way. Come on."

She shoved him out of the room long enough for her to quickly wash and throw on the clothes she'd had the foresight to lay out the night before. She could hear him practically chomping at the bit just outside, as if this was some sort of adventure, a test of his abilities that he looked forward to.

"What about Charlene?" she asked as she emerged, still only half buttoned and snapped. She couldn't see Charlene looking forward to this at all.

"She'll be out. Pauline knows where we're going to be and she promised to drop Charlene off later." He tucked her hand, and the boots she hadn't had time to put on, under his arm, escorting her down the hallway firmly, giving her no time for anything but a quick wave to Pauline, seated alone at the breakfast table.

"I can't just leave her without a proper hello, Turner," she protested as he opened the Bronco door and put both her and a bag full of supplies inside.

"If I gave you the time to say a proper hello, she'd never let you say a proper good-bye. She'd have you feeling so guilty inside of five minutes that you'd be miserable all day, if you even came. I've found that short, sweet good-byes are the best, a lesson you could learn from. But if it's worrying you, don't let it. She'll be around long before the day is done to check up on you."

"Turner, you have a large unemotional, uncaring streak."

"It's more than a streak. It runs through and through and goes hand in hand with my sense of self-preservation."

She sighed. The argument wasn't worth it. What was it to her if he didn't know how to bend, if he couldn't empathize with other people's pain, other people's needs, and perhaps soften his own stand a little for anyone else's benefit? She wouldn't have to deal with him at all within a few weeks. That thought brought a funny pang of regret. She pushed it aside, pulling her mind back to the problems and the situation at hand.

"Did you check the first aid kit? Do we have more than one snake bite kit? It's too hot for them now out in the open, but we're going to be inside a lot of cool places and scrambling around the rocks they hide under. And what about the extra fuel . . . and the water? And did you remember to pack your backpack with enough emergency rations?"

The engine revved into life. "Trust me."

Her hand still remained on the door latch. She should check to make sure...

"Are you coming with me or aren't you? Or is this just an excuse to go back to Pauline?"

She opened the door and slammed it hard, settling back in the seat with a tightly drawn mouth. "You're never going to live it down, Turner Jameson, if we get out there and we've forgotten anything."

"I'm a man who enjoys taking risks now and then. I like life's little challenges."

Not reassured, she peered over the back seat once they were under way, trying to see what they were missing and what they might need. How could she trust a city person in the first place to know what was needed to survive in the desert? And how could she trust Turner who made her feel defensive far more often than he made her feel secure? And, where were they going? She didn't even know that.

"Where's the map?" She'd see for herself.

He handed her a sandwich wrapped in wax paper.

"Okay, but what's the scale of miles and what is it a map of? Are these mountains?"

"No. They're sesame seeds, and that's your breakfast. Open it, it's good."

She took the sandwich. "I am not amused. And I'm not a child, so I wish you'd stop the orders."

He veered off the road onto the sand, seemingly unconcerned that there were no civilized landmarks to guide his course.

"No? I apologize then. Pauline orders your life so much, I thought you must enjoy it."

Something green oozed out of the sandwich and stuck to the wax paper as she impulsively hit him with it. The reason for her temper vanished, escaping her as she inspected the French bread and whatever else sandwich.

"It's green. God, have I killed it or was it always like this? What is it?"

"Avocado, bacon, mushroom, and onion."

"That's disgusting." She enclosed the "food" in a paper bag at her feet. "And you said to trust you. I'll bet you didn't eat yours."

"No, I didn't," he admitted readily. "But then I got up early enough to make bacon and eggs and hash browns, all the good stuff, before it was time to go. You didn't."

"You could have gotten me up."

"You ordered me out of your bedroom, if I remember correctly. Besides, I did try, but I couldn't get past your watch dog until she went down to have breakfast herself and by then it was too late."

"Pauline?" she asked, already sure that it was. "She wouldn't let you come in because she assumed your motives would be dishonorable." She was only half teasing.

"She didn't like what she assumed my motives were for being there. She thought I only wanted to wake you up so that we could go off and study the mines. You must know she doesn't want you anywhere near the mines. Though I don't suppose she would have approved of my real motives for being there an hour earlier than I was there, either." He grinned at her suggestively.

"You're awful." She was not going to take him or his leering, humorous grins seriously at this time of the morning.

"On the contrary. I've been told that I'm rather exceptional." He smiled at the look she threw him. "Look." He pointed to Teresa's Jeep and Gerry's Land Rover, small colored dots parked on a tan backdrop in the distance, observable mainly because of the sun that glinted brightly off their windshields. "And I'm not a bad tracker, either. It's good to know I haven't lost my touch."

The tiny figures grew larger until she could make out Teresa and Gerry working at something beside the vehicles and Indian, sitting in the shade of a rock overhang. Turner eased the Bronco in alongside.

"Morning," he greeted them robustly. "Is this our

work party and have you been waiting long?"

"Yes, it is, and we just got here." Teresa handed a steaming cup of coffee to him and one to Honey, too. "But we're all ready to go to work whenever you are."

Indian joined them. Honey observed wryly that they looked like walking advertisements from a hiking gear catalog. Turner had made a transformation, too, and *looked* the part as much as they did, having altered yet another aspect of his present lifestyle. She could only hope he was as well prepared underneath his fine feathers, and though the others looked to him for instructions, she couldn't help but feel a certain apprehension.

"We've got a lot of ground to cover," he stated, at once business-like. "Over sixty mines that lie within the boundaries of the park that we know of, and I need photos of each one, both inside and out, as well as directions on how to get to them that anyone will understand and be able to follow. I'll need exact measurements of the ground outside and at least some rudimentary measurements and diagrams of what the inside layout is. I'll need timber samples and I'll need a write-up of the history of each mine, as much as anyone knows, including any call-outs you might have had in them."

"Is *that* all?" Teresa shrugged eloquently. "We should be done by sundown at the latest. Seriously though Turner, how long did you plan to stay here in Pahrump? I hope you like the desert in winter."

"There is a lot to do. But we'll get more accomplished, I'm sure, if everyone chooses a task before we start. There's enough to do so that if each of us picks something to be responsible for, it'll go faster and smoother."

"Good." Teresa voiced her preference at once. "I don't know about the rest of you, but my expertise in dealing with the mines has always been with backup procedures. I left all the below ground work to those who knew and liked what they were doing."

"Gerry?" Turner queried.

"I'm better topside," he admitted somewhat apologetically. "You see, we all had to learn the basics, but because of our limited number, everyone had to specialize. Honey and Daryl, as a team, were our mine rescue team."

"Don't apologize." Turner fit them to their various choices without taking a further consensus. "I'm going to have to learn from all of you. Why don't you and Teresa divide the above-ground work to be done between you. I'll try to insist that Charlene is around to give you another hand. I've done quite a bit of amateur rock climbing, and I've done a bit of extra research on mine rescue, so I'll probably be the most effective there, along with Indian and, of course, Honey." He stopped while Honey held her breath. "That is, Indian, unless you'd prefer not to go into the mines?"

"Doesn't matter," Indian responded. "I'm easy."

No one had asked what she might prefer, Honey reflected. No one had considered that she might not want to step foot inside a mine again, under the circumstances. But could she really consider *not* going along with Turner's plan? She couldn't, in all conscience, allow Indian and Turner to handle the tricky mine situations that often cropped up alone, when she was the only one with any real training and experience. She shivered under the warm sun. But, oh, how hard that might prove to be. She directed a hesitant look in the mines' direction. They looked innocuous enough from this distance. Three in a row, all at the base of a low, red rock mountain. The first had caved in entirely, leaving only a small, waste rock-filled crater to show anything had ever been there. The second one, some twenty-five feet from the first, must be connected somewhere underground, but it, too, was only partially opened, its entrance half sealed with crumbling rocks from the mountainside and sand that had blown in to cover the decaying support beams. It did not look safe to enter, despite the animal trails leading into it. But it was neither of these that caused her misgiving. It was the third mine; part of the mountain itself, it must once have been a cave, for the entry way was unshored and looked to be made of solid rock. Moreover, its mouth was very wide, the darkness from within like a black hole in outer space, gobbling up any light from outside. It held a dark fascination that both horrified her and told her too that it would hold an almost irresistible allure for teenage rock hounds and simply curious. It looked safe enough from the outside to make them forgetful and unwary of any shaft that might, and that indeed almost surely did, lie somewhere just beyond sight inside.

No one spoke, an unnatural hush settling over them all as they drew closer. No choice but to follow, Honey clenched her hands tightly, hiding them in the pockets of her pants.

A sudden dust devil swirled sand around them and into the aperture in the earth, the echoing sound of the breeze within the cavern like some awful and hungry animal waiting inside to devour them. She wiped at the cold sweat that had gathered on her face, and hoped no one else would notice her growing apprehension, glad that she hadn't eaten the sandwich lest it be rejected by the nervous churnings of her stomach.

"Steady on, Honey," she lectured herself silently. "It's an inanimate thing, this mine. It won't reach out and bite you. It can't hurt you if you're very, very careful." She whispered the words to herself as an incantation against evil.

The drop in temperature just inside the entrance was dramatic, and she had to clench her teeth together to keep them from chattering.

"Are we all ready to get started?" Turner looked to each of them, so confident, so sure of himself and his safety, trusting the mine floor and ceiling to stay in their respective proper places.

"I'm ready." She shook off her fear. It would get better. It would have to. Didn't they say if one fell off a horse, one had to get right back in the saddle again? Well, she was eighteen months overdue for this particular saddle, for this particular ride, but if she could get through this one mine, she thought she could manage the rest. "I'm ready," she repeated with emphasis.

The others fanned out, more than happy to leave the underground work to Honey and Turner, Indian with a tape measure, Gerry with a camera of the instant-picture variety, and Teresa following close behind with a notepad and pencil. They didn't know how she was feeling inside, didn't know that she hadn't been inside a mine since the accident had happened. She had kept that secret along with her fears and her pain locked up where they couldn't be seen, where they might just dry up and go away if she ignored them long enough. But she hadn't counted on having to go into the mines at all, assuming that Turner would just want to nose around the outside, assure himself that it *was* there and potentially dangerous, and leave well enough alone. He did not leave well enough alone; she wondered briefly if he ever did, or if he made it a point to push himself and step over the lines of safety, caution, good sense and good manners.

She hooked herself, as he did, to the, insofar as she was concerned, tenuous safety line, and took the cold metal object he placed in her hand.

"Do you know what it's for?" he asked.

She rechecked the harness that was attached to the line. "Of course." She was frightened, but not forgetful. "It's a sniffer. It emits a signal if it detects any of several toxic gasses."

"You do know your stuff." He nodded his approval. "I was beginning to wonder if you had relied on Daryl for all the expertise, too. You're white as a sheet and I don't want to be responsible for anyone who doesn't know what they're doing. I'm too unfamiliar with the exact procedures of all this myself."

She walked slowly back into the mine, forcing him to follow her for a change. "I did rely on Daryl. But I've probably got more experience than anyone else around here in going into the mines. *I* know what *I'm* doing. Do you?" Put *him* on the defensive.

"I'll guess we'll find out."

Lord save her from any more accidents. She sent the

prayer up and swept past him before he had an accident that proved his guess wrong, snapping her head lamp on to see where she was leading him. Even with his light, as he drew abreast of her, the cavern was dark, the light from the outside refusing to filter in this far or illuminate the rather large main room more than a little bit. Honey kept her eyes to the floor, strewn with waste rock, her nerves stretched to the breaking point, knowing in her mind that the main vertical shaft was still probably some distance ahead of them, yet keeping an illogical eye on the floor just in case it had moved from where their information told them it was.

"Tell me what you know about this mine."

The question distracted her from her observation of the floor, and she wondered if he had asked it for precisely that reason.

"It dates back to 1880. Someone found ore in the cave and dug further back in hopes they'd find more. They did; but when the ore grew hard to reach and not profitable to mine here, they sunk two more shafts to see if they could follow the vein out, see if it widened. It apparently didn't do them much good because the whole thing was closed down just a few years later.

"So it's old." He ran his hand along the rock wall banded in various colors. "But it looks safe enough."

"*That's* why it is so dangerous. It looks safe, but it isn't. People rarely go into mines that are obviously dangerous." She slowed her pace. "The floor slopes downward here, see? Can you feel it?"

"I can feel it." He walked on steadily, showing none of the faltering that she did. "Where's the shaft from here?"

"Another twenty feet or so ahead of us." She hung back. "The floor slants gradually here, but if I recall . . . I was in here once before . . . a long time ago . . . Just a little way ahead the pitch is much, much steeper on our side and it would be easy to slide in. There are no hand holds and there's lots of gravel."

"And on the other side?"

"Level . . . or almost. They took the ore out from the

side, wore an incline into the dirt and rock."

"Good, because I want to take a look in the shaft to see if I can judge how deep it might be. I'll do it from the other side."

"Are you crazy?" The cry was torn from her throat without thought.

"No." He did an about face, ahead of her and stopped in the middle of the tunnel. "I'm here for an investigation, remember?"

"No, I forgot. We're here on an afternoon outing," she said sarcastically.

"I'm going to have to get a ball park estimate of the shaft's depth, and if there's timber on the sides, I'll need a sample of that, too. I can't do either of those things from here."

He tried to walk away from her but she caught hold of his safety line, and refused to let it go. "Brother, you are so damned nonchalant. Why are you wearing this if there's no danger?"

"A precaution."

"It's dangerous, dangerous, dangerous! Can't you see that?" She pleaded with him, her eyes wide with anxiety.

"I've told you before, Honey, I need proof."

"Damn your proof!" She held the line in her hands so tightly, it cut little lines into her flesh. "Don't play macho man with me; I can't take it. Don't go near that shaft, please." She added the please, a last embellishment hopefully. "For me, please don't."

"For you, yes. For one thing, to show you that this is not one of life's impossibilities, and to show you that you can't stop taking the risks of living just because you're preoccupied with death. But more than that, I have to go for me. It's a part of my job. And I won't have you thinking you can let our relationship affect the decisions I have to make concerning this investigation."

"We don't have a relationship. I'm not speaking as . . . as whatever it is you think I am. I'm speaking as a rational, trained individual whom you ought to listen to for your own safety."

"You're speaking to me as someone who cares a hell

of a lot more about me than she cares to admit, and I appreciate that, but I'm still going to do this."

She let the line slip and watched as he tred a cat-walk of earth and rock beside the shaft, making his way around it.

"If you hadn't cared about me and my safety so much," he continued talking to her in a normal tone of voice as he tiptoed around the shaft, "you'd never have come this far into the mine, because it scares you a great deal. But you've got guts." He smiled at her from the other side of the shaft. "I like a woman with guts, and that's why I'm not giving in to your fears, and it's why I'm not giving up on you, and it is also why I'm going to ask you to do one thing more for me. I need you to come on over and give me a hand."

"I'm not getting any closer, so you can forget about that." She was convinced of it. Insanity wasn't catching.

"Then I'll have to do it alone."

Or was it? He seemed not to notice her quick intake of breath as he positioned himself on his stomach next to the hole, reaching down into it with a tape measure.

"I can't feel the bottom." He inched closer.

"No, just a minute. I'm coming over." She amended her earlier argument, but it was an insanity that was against her will.

"I'll turn on a larger light." The hand-held, battery-operated lantern shone brightly and fought back the eerie darkness that was below far more effectively than either of their head lamps had. She reached the side, a midway point between her side and his, along the catwalk. And it was at this point that the light caught on and reflected back up a shape of something dangling from a ledge within the shaft, something long and white, a skeleton half buried and dangling, poised on the edge of infinity.

A thin, high pitched wail rent the silence of their small cavity, a terrified, disbelieving sound that came from her own throat. She flattened herself against the wall, cling-ing to it with her fingernails lest the vertigo that attacked her senses dropped her into the pit along with it.

"Honey! Honey, it's all right. It looks like an animal. A coyote."

The words meant nothing. She could not move, her whole being numb and unresponsive. The wall, the ledge she stood on, was the only solid sure thing in her existence and she had no intention of leaving it.

She was only vaguely aware of Turner as he moved around the shaft, coming slowly, oh, so slowly, closer to her, his hands on her safety rope holding tightly, his voice low and soothing.

"It's okay, Honeysuckle. It's all right little desert flower. I'm almost there." His voice rose for just a second. "No! Don't look down! It's okay. Look at me. That's right. I told you you could rely on me, I said you could trust me. Trust me, Honey. Don't move."

She did as she was told, some inner voice urging her to listen to the reason behind that voice, until he was inches from her and he catapulted them both to the ground away from the shaft.

She was in his arms then and he was on his feet, taking her away from the horror in the excavation. When he finally stopped running, they were a few yards from the outside.

She clung to his neck, to the security he had promised, and before she could think whether it was right or wrong, she clung to his lips, drawing him closer with her arms that held him tight, drawing them both to the mine floor until his body covered hers and they were both tangled in a spaghetti of ropes. Her body molded itself to his in a desire to get closer to him and away from everything else. She could feel each muscle as he moved against her, and when she eventually released him, she could feel his warm breathing, so gloriously alive, against her cheek. It was good to be held again and not be so alone . . .

"Turner? Honey? Are you two in here?" Teresa stood framed in sunlight in the cave doorway, a hand full of photographs. She stopped in embarrassment, standing still before them until her eyes adjusted to the dim mine light. "I'm sorry. I didn't realize..."

"Honey had a bit of a scare," he explained coolly. "She'll be fine if you'd just give us a minute."

"Ah...sure. I'll wait outside." Teresa beat a hasty retreat, leaving them in an uncomfortable silence, the moment they had shared gone.

"I don't know what you must be thinking." Honey got up stiffly and wiped at a strand of hair that had gotten loose from the clips that held it in check. "I've never lost control like that before. I am very sorry. It was my fault. It's just that I..."

He finished for her, the words coming out in short choppy bites. "It's just that you were scared out of your wits before we even came into the mine and when we saw the coyote skeleton, your imagination took over and you turned to me for comfort." He let go of a long held breath and snapped his head lamp off, preferring the semidarkness. "I knew...or at least I suspected that you hadn't gone into many, if any mines, since Daryl's accident."

Her face was troubled and the light on her helmet streaked back and forth across the walls as she shook her head in confusion. "You didn't say anything."

"I thought it might just be the catalyst you needed, show you once and for all that a mine is just a place, not necessarily to be dreaded in all instances."

"You aren't going to change my mind on that score."

"Then I can't continue to take you with me on this. I can't afford to let anything happen to you."

"No, you can't do that!" She couldn't keep the note of fearful pleading from her expression. "You can't leave me behind now."

He covered the short distance between them in two strides and moved his hands as if to put them about her waist, but stopped, waiting for the answer to a question as yet unasked.

"Why? Why are you asking me, now, not to leave you behind?"

"Because if you can't see, by now, that you're investigating something that could be responsible for your death at any time, I can't allow you to go on alone. I won't be responsible for your death. I won't be responsible for a mine taking *another* life. I couldn't bear that."

The hope, the momentary anticipation faded from his face, to be replaced by a bleak, forced impartiality.

"The only hope I have of convincing you," she rattled on, "is to come along."

"You could be right." He did his best to look uncaring. "You might be able to convince me, and by rights, admitting that, I should send you right now."

"You can't." She wished it aloud.

"No, I can't. I don't think I could let you go now, even if you wanted to go. Is that what you wanted to hear?"

She remembered the emotional kiss, trying to recall the exact feeling that had prompted her to give it. What *did* she want?

"I don't know," she answered him truthfully. "All I *do* know is that I have to come with you. I have a part to play in this investigation, and I can't begin to put the past and all the fears that go with it behind me until it's over." She turned the tables on him again. "Is *that* what you wanted to hear?"

"*No.*" His voice was cryptic. "But it's a start."

CHAPTER SIX

TURNER REMAINED BELOW in the mine when she left, her place taken by Indian who wouldn't come completely unglued at life's little unexpected surprises. She leaned against the rock face in which the mine had been cut, allowing her body's suppressed trembling to take over for a few moments. She'd made such a fool of herself, probably losing what small credibility Turner had given her. And it wasn't only her reaction to the mines, which, now that this experience was over, hopefully would resume a proper perspective. It was the way she had literally thrown herself at him after denying that she wanted anything to do with him earlier. He would think he was dealing with an emotional basket case. She touched her full lips with the feel of his kiss still tingling there, wondering herself just how emotionally stable she could be.

"Did you get thrown out of paradise?"

"Paradise?" Honey had sensed Teresa's soft-footed approach, but couldn't make sense out of her question.

"Yeah." She dropped a friendly arm around Honey's shoulder in sisterly comaraderie. "You know, for tasting the forbidden fruit."

"I didn't get thrown out. I left under my own steam, but you've got the forbidden part right." She managed a shaky laugh.

"It's only forbidden if you think it is." Teresa daisy-chained the slack safety line into neat coils and slung it over her shoulder. "There's nothing wrong with what I saw. You're both single and young..."

"Don't. Don't start." Honey gave her a look designed to stop the onslaught of logic. "I don't want to hear it."

"Whether you want to hear it or not, it's true," Teresa insisted. "He's attracted to you, I can tell. You're attracted to him; I can tell that, too. You're working *together* on this mine thing now, not against each other. So why can't you be close?"

For one, Honey wasn't so sure they *were* working together, and two, she was not yet free.

"Honey, are you listening to me?" Teresa dropped the ropes in the Bronco. "I was asking you why you couldn't be close. After all, if I can't have him, there's no reason why you shouldn't."

Anything to get Teresa's mind off the one-track subject. "Oh? Are you tossing in the towel?"

The plump brunette blushed, Honey apparently hitting on a subject purely by accident that her friend did not want to discuss to death. "I think I might have other interests. But what's stopping you?"

"I can think of two things right off the top of my head." Honey squinted at the sunlight that glinted off Pauline's car just pulling up.

"What?"

"Not what—who! Look." She tilted her head to indicate Pauline, seated behind the wheel, and Charlene, just getting out. She would have been quite the style at a southern California poolside cocktail party where her thin sandals could be decorative and not have to cope with anything more rugged than dichondra, and her sleek tanned body could be protected by an umbrella. But the pale yellow halter top and short shorts she wore weren't going to do much to protect her from the sun here. She wasn't wearing a hat, and, if she should get lost, she'd blend in with the sand from top to bottom, making herself impossible to locate.

Yes, Charlene could be a deterrent to any relationship Turner and she might think of having. That was a reason to keep her within sight at all times.

"Where's Turner?" Charlene had no time for small talk, and Honey could see her diplomatic intentions fall by the wayside.

"The third mine." She indicated the general direction. "But I need to talk with you first because you're going to have to go back with Pauline and change."

"Change? Why?"

"Well . . . because you're dressed all wrong to spend any time in the desert."

"You're right." Charlene did not seem in the least worried. "Look, nothing personal," she explained. "You look like you were dressed in garage sale leavings, and you seem to have convinced Turner to temporarily go back to his roots, too, but I'm not dressing like that, and I'm not going to go native just because Turner has something to prove to himself."

"This has nothing to do with Turner, honestly," Honey tried to explain.

"On the contrary, it has everything to do with Turner." Charlene spoke with all the confidence of one who knows that what she says is the truth. "Do you think they usually send men of Turner's caliber and experience out on routine field work? They don't. He's worth his weight in gold in executive administration and they pay him just about that much to do what he usually does for them. But he's been . . . restless . . . lately and when he got your letter he took it into his head to come out and do the investigation himself. Oh, he's thorough all right, and as objective and hard-nosed as they come, but he wouldn't need to do all the leg work himself. He could hire others to bring the information in for him. But he doesn't want to. He wants to do it himself. He's got this crazy idea that this is the only thing he's ever failed at; managing to make it, whatever that means, in Pahrump. And so he's blown it all out of proportion. It's become the only thing of importance to him."

"I didn't know. I thought he had come here, like I said, just to supervise the closing of the mines."

Charlene lit a cigarette and studied her. "You enter into it somehow. I'm not sure. I'm not at all sure what he wants to find here, what he needs to prove, but I'm here to see that he doesn't lose his perspective altogether. I'm going to try to get him to come back early and let someone else take over. What I am not going to do is cater to his obsession with this place." She ground the cigarette out into the sand. "I'm a reminder of the world he really lives in, and I don't intend to change and blend in with the rest of you."

Honey watched her walk off with a great deal less fear than Honey herself had shown upon nearing the mines. The dangers posed by the mines *were* real. Why couldn't she make anyone understand that? You couldn't play at "King-of-the-Mountain" on a mountain liable to fall in on you, no matter what you had to prove or who you had to convince. And she could just see Charlene and her wobbly little sandals blithely tripping down the corridors of the third mine, a disaster waiting to happen. She'd have to go after her...

"Honey?" Pauline's voice broke in on her intentions, her blond-gray head thrust from the driver's side of the car. "I need to speak to you for a moment, dear."

"Yes, Pauline. What is it?" She did her best to soften the impatient irritation that had crept into her voice.

"Dear, I was hoping I could persuade you to forget this mine business and come back into town with me. Ms. Mercer assures me that there's no need for you to be here, that she and Turner can handle the rest of the investigation on their own. I'm sure Daryl wouldn't want you to be out here. Please."

Honey took her eyes from the older woman's face

which, from the sound of her voice, was pitiful indeed
and apt to make her feel guiltier than she did already.

"Mother..." She used the endearment purposely,
speaking gently. "Ms. Mercer doesn't have one iota of
an idea of how much work we have to do. Turner needs
me...needs my help. I can't abandon him now just
because you'd like me to. And Ms. Mercer wouldn't
know how to deal with a pothole, let alone a mine shaft,
and, so you see, he's going to need me more than ever,
just to keep an eye on her. Can you understand that?"

"I just feel so abandoned." Pauline looked older and
more fragile than Honey liked to think of her as being.

"I'm not abandoning you permanently, but I do have
to go now. There are things I have to do." She waved
a good-bye to Pauline who still watched in her rearview
mirror, and turned her back on the sight. She stopped
swiftly and looked around, a mother hen who notices
one of her chicks has gone only by the absence of it's
incessant chirping.

"Where has that woman gone?" She demanded aloud
to the cactus who kept their own counsel. The mouth of
the third cave was empty. If she'd actually gone inside,
without waiting for her or Turner as escort...She started
to run, calling Charlene's name out louder in between
breaths. "Charlene!"

She was rewarded at last, but not by Charlene's answer to her call. It was Turner, and he did not sound
pleased.

"She's over here," he shouted, even though she had
come within normal tone of voice range. "Where is your
head, woman? Don't you know you can't let untrained
people go about unescorted around these mines? When
I heard her and came out, she was only feet from this."
He prodded a shallowly indented ditch next to the mine
with a thin length of pipe designed for that purpose. The
ditch grew deeper, very quickly, the soil and the sand
swallowed up inside an ever enlarging canal.

"Unshored tunneling from mine three." He looked at
her critically.

She didn't appreciate the reprimand. If Charlene

hadn't gone off on her own in the first place, it wouldn't have happened.

"I apologize. What do you want me to do now that you have Ms. Mercer safely in your hands?" The subtle sarcasm helped clarify her state of mind, a healthy dose of righteous indignation dispelling the other unsettling emotions.

"I've got all the samples and measurements I need from mine three, so I don't need you here," he responded curtly. "See if you can give the others a hand with the remaining two. By the way, I've scheduled three more mine sites for today so we'd better try to act as a unit and get back to work. We can't afford any more delays or unprofessionalism."

She turned a pair of amber snake eyes on him. That was a low blow. "Whatever you say," she returned sweetly. "I'll just help the others tie up loose ends and leave all the professional decisions to you."

She turned her back on them both and with a chin high, made for one of the other mines, keeping her gate steady and slow. If he wanted her out of the way, fine. If he wanted to run the show, fine. If he wanted to prove something to himself . . . well, he'd have to prove something to her as well!

"We'll just see how good at administration and organization he really is."

"What?" Gerry lifted his bright blond head and allowed the measuring tape to snap back into its case, done with the job.

"Nothing, Gerry. I was talking to myself."

"There's no need to do that. Come talk to me." He jotted measurements down onto a notepad. "That is, if you don't mind talking while I work."

"No. Actually, that's why I'm here. I came to give you a hand. I'm not working with Turner now, so I thought—"

"You two sure strike sparks off each other, don't you?"

"Yes," she confirmed. "Maybe it's a competition to

see who's boss, to see who of us is the stronger, who has the most power over the actions of the other. I don't know, that could sound ridiculous to you. Anyway, I think I've lost the battle."

"A clear cut case of too many chiefs and not enough Indians as far as I'm concerned," Gerry assured her.

"Did you call me?" Indian walked over questioningly to them and set the pouch of timber samples down on the ground.

"Nope." Honey straightened herself up from Gerry. "But you must have E.S.P. because I was just going to call you. Gerry is working partners with Teresa. Can I work with you?"

"That's why I volunteered." He handed her the timber and ore samples and she followed him to the Jeep. He was someone steady to hold onto when everyone else and everything else was crumbling in on her. She was glad to be working with him again.

"Ready for a break?" Indian called to her from a hole in the face of a cliff some twenty feet up, and began the descent, refusing to use the safety line and harness Turner had rigged for him, his fingers and moccasined toes clinging to the curves and creases like a lizard. Honey stood back to give him the room he needed to climb down and sat down next to him as he let go and slid to a squatting position in the sand.

"Want some water?" She handed her canteen to him.

"No." He opened a leather pouch and moved the tied plastic baggies of wood slivers and tiny rocks aside and pulled out a Coors beer, popping the top off and spraying them both with warm beer.

"How you can drink that stuff I'll never know. Uggh!" She made a face as he drank thirstily from the can.

"It takes a real man to drink warm beer," he said. "Squaws don't."

She took the can from his hand, and, mentally holding her nose, took a swig.

"But then you never were like most women." He used

the more respectful term to describe her sex. "Most women I know don't work as hard as me," he boasted. "But you . . . you got spunk. Going in that mine today took spunk; and before you had it, too. I remember when you first came to Pahrump, when Daryl brought you. You didn't know how to work a farm, run a cotton-picking machine, a bailer or a tractor, but you learned."

"I almost ran over you with that tractor, do you remember?" She leaned against him and rested her head on his shoulder, content to let the tension wash from her bones and lay in the sunshine of the late afternoon.

"I thought to myself . . ." He continued: "I thought, how can a woman who works like a man, still be so much of a woman?"

"I worked at it. It took getting up an hour early before everyone else to moisturize my skin and do my hair. I think I worked at that more than I did on the ranch doing your so-called man's work." The memory faded painfully. "I'm afraid it's a skill I've lost."

"You still look pretty good to me." He peered down at her slim legs and rounded hips in the cotton jeans. "Very womanly."

"Maybe on the outside, but it's not the same. I don't feel that way on the inside any more. Not since . . ."

"Hogwash." He brushed her self-pity aside. "How can you not be what you are, not feel what it is natural and normal for a woman to feel? It's like, if I suddenly no longer felt Indian . . . would I still not be Indian?"

"How can one person ask so many questions when we have so much work to do?"

The old man squinted up at the sun sliding lower against the western horizon. "You young people . . . you and Turner both . . . constantly denying what you are, pretending to be something you are not. Just because you have been successful at the game you think the pretending is real. I tell you it's not, and you will find that you cannot keep the truth from yourself forever . . . either of you."

"The only truth I know is that I'm beat." She had no

arguments, only evasions. "How about quitting?"

Dusk was on them before they climbed to rejoin the others at the cars.

"Look, I'm so dirty I'm the same color as the sand." Honey inspected herself in the Bronco's side mirror.

"I'm so covered with dirt Gerry tried to stuff me in an ore sample bag, only I wouldn't fit," Teresa boasted, adding to their dirty one upmanship.

Gerry chuckled and leaned over to brush the dirt from his hair.

"Dandruff." His eyes flashed up in surprise. "Though I'd say we four have gotten off light."

Teresa whistled in sympathy as Turner and Charlene approached. Working furiously all day to cover the ground he had set for them, no one had noticed as Charlene's fair complexion reddened under the blazing sun until it now all but glowed with radiant, sunburnt heat. She walked as if each step hurt, and she carried one sandal by a broken strap. They could hear her plaintive whine yards away.

"I *did* use a sunscreen, Turner, and it happened anyway. Look at me," she demanded. "And I'll roast alive if I cover up like you all do. How can you take it?"

"I was raised here. I guess it's in the blood. It didn't take me long to get acclimated again."

"You'd be too stubborn to admit otherwise, even if it were true. Don't get too used to it, will you? I'd like to get back home while I still have some skin left."

"Home?" He looked at Honey and the others against the sand and sagebrush and cactus backdrop. "We'll see." He addressed them then. "How did we do?"

"That depends on what stick you use to measure us with." Gerry crossed his arms assessing their situation. "We've certainly got far more accomplished than's been done in previous years. It's a start."

"Not much more though." Teresa had set herself up as the pessimist in their midst. "How long do you plan to stay here?"

"I don't have a firm schedule. Why?"

Teresa looked to them all for support. "We've all worked hard today, and it's taken us all day long to do six mine sites, three of which were at one location. The way I figure it, unless we get more help, which you can kiss good-bye if past experience is any indication, or unless we work half the night besides, we're going to be at this every day for the next couple of weeks."

So much for Charlene's hasty retreat. She groaned and wrapped ice from their propane powered small cooler into a towel and placed it on her legs. "Enough is enough. Turner, all you're doing is proving what a masochist you are *and* we are for agreeing to it."

He frowned at her, then acknowledged her point with a small grunt. "I know. I can't ask you all to work nonstop for two weeks on this."

"Or more," Teresa reminded him.

There was an uncomfortable silence as each delved into their reasons for volunteering in the first place and how strong their conviction was to stick with it.

"It's not the work we mind so much," Gerry said finally. "Really it's to our benefit when . . . that is, if the mines are closed. It'll save us leg work and uncountable call-outs at a later time. Personally I'd rather do it now, when there isn't a life at stake. It's just that for me, and I know for Teresa, too, we've both taken time off our regular jobs for this, and it isn't an indefinite leave. We've got people to cover for us, but only for so long."

"He's right. We can manage for a week, maybe stretch it into two, but that's about all," Teresa pronounced the judgment matter of factly.

There didn't seem to be a way to factor the equation of work and time limits to a better solution.

"We'll have to cross our fingers then that everything works like clockwork . . . of a fast clock."

But Turner hadn't counted on all of the problems over which faith, hope, and crossed fingers had no control whatsoever, like tires that went flat, and tools that broke, or mines that were as inaccessible as it was possible to be. Just when they decided that no one, but no one would be foolish enough to enter, the side of a beer can would catch their eye and change their minds. Concealed in beds of cactus, some were unapproachable looking enough to make all wish they hadn't tried, but not so sheltered that, once inside, evidence cropped up to convince them that someone had gotten in, from soda cans to snake skins, from discarded clothes to worse.

Honey shuddered and looked around the floor of the particular mine she'd commandeered for its shade, just to make sure she wasn't sharing the space with a reptile or two, the only things that rattled her about mines any more. With constant exposure, she had settled down, her half logical, half irrational fears had been replaced by the weary monotony of repeated entrances and evidence gathering. Her only real fears now, besides the odd snake, ironically were that she, or more correctly Turner, wouldn't be able to enter and investigate enough mines in the time left to them.

"Speak of the devil . . ." She invited a stubble-bearded Turner into her sanctuary, moving over to give him a less lumpy spot in the sand.

"Feel like some company?"

"Who's taking her to town now, and for what this time?" She didn't need to ask why he was here. He rarely left Charlene's side if she was around the mines, a place she seemed to prefer avoiding at all costs, apparently inventing excuses to absent herself by having one or more of them take her into town.

"How'd you know?" He couldn't hide his surprise.

"I saw the Land Rover leave." She was in no mood for polite platitudes. "Besides, you never let her out of your sight unless she has another keeper."

That elicited a smile, the first she had seen in days. "I don't dare. The woman's a menace. She does fine on taxis, she doesn't get lost on freeways or at shopping malls or cocktail parties, and I'll swear she's the best assistant I've ever had, bar none. But here—"

"She's a menace." They spoke at once, a two-part

harmony that eased the tension that had blanketed them for days.

"It's difficult for her here," he felt obliged to explain in her defense. "It's as alien as another planet for her."

"You aren't used to it either..." She did not finish the argument. "Or have you reverted back to what Indian so fondly refers to as your natural state?" She reached over tentatively to touch his sun bronzed arm that extended from a carelessly rolled up work shirt sleeve. "I'd hardly recognize you as the same man who stepped out of the Mercedes a week or so ago. You're dressed differently... like us, you have relearned, I have to admit, how to coexist with our desert without destroying it... as we have, you work with us, talk about the same things. You *could* be one of us if you weren't so eager to return to the city."

"What makes you so sure I'm eager to leave?"

"Charlene says you are. And you are in a hurry to finish this project."

He shrugged. "We've already voted that Charlene doesn't know everything. As to the other, the only one who wants to spend the rest of the summer out here is Indian."

"Okay." She conceded the point to him. "But you don't want to stay after this is over, do you? I mean, for all the show of getting back to nature and all that you left behind here fifteen years ago, underneath that sandy exterior there's still the man who gets his hair cut by a stylist and who buys his suits from a tailor and who shops at I. Magnin's rather than the thrift shops, right?"

"Curious little thing, aren't you?" He played with the waste rock and sand at their feet, piling it into miniature mountains while he talked. "Did you ever think the two might be compatible? The man who came here and the town he came to? Or that the man driving the Mercedes was really someone else, someone entirely different underneath?"

"But could you stay after being away that long; and living here as long as you did, how could you leave?"

"Maybe I don't have the same incentives as you do to stay. The desert, any small town I suppose, can be very lonely. At least the city offers...diversions."

He sounded sincere though Honey had trouble imagining him ever feeling alone. There must be countless women willing to share his time.

"I'm alone, too, and yet I want to stay."

His eyes flashed a warning. "Do you *want* to stay or are you forced to stay?"

She got up from the cave floor, leaving her comfortable position, no longer so comfortable. "I'm not tied here. I love it here, the ruggedness of it, the wild beauty, the starkness of the land that still lives under the adverse conditions. It's a part of me, of what I am, like a piece of my own body. I'd never want to leave it, Turner, and that's the truth."

"I envy you." He got up and stood behind her to stare out of the mine entrance and at the land. "I feel about this desert as I always did, akin to what you say you feel. It has the same draw on me. I think I could make it here, too, but it isn't enough."

"What more do you want?" To add anything of his world to this desert would destroy what it was.

"I need someone to share it with me." He tilted her chin around so that he could see her eyes. "Don't you ever need anyone, Honey? A flesh and blood man to share this with, the loves and the dreams you have about all this? Doesn't all the desolation you see remind you of the emptiness you carry inside?" There was an ache somewhere deep within him that fought to come out, but could not quite, answered by an ever so tiny voice crying out in mutual need inside her.

"Yes," she whispered simply. Only that need did not make her want to leave the desert, it made her want someone to come and share it with her. She enfolded him in her arms, holding him, relishing the silent communication that flowed between them. To love this man, to be loved by him and share their common dreams...She contemplated that ecstacy for a brief moment.

"Honey, are you through loafing up there yet?" Gerry stood at the base of the cactus patch surrounding their fortress-like mine.

Turner did not relinquish his hold on her, his breathing almost hypnotic. "Did you hear anything?"

"Birds?" she offered.

The voice called again, joined this time by a female warbler.

"We could have more anonymity in the city than we ever do in this whole damned deserted desert, you know?"

"Maybe it's better this way, Turner."

"Better for who?" he demanded, the warmth gone from his features. "Certainly not for you or for me." But he took her hand, despite the reluctance to leave, and pulled her out of the mine and down, less careful of the cactus spines under foot than she would have liked.

"What's so important?" He must have sounded as irritable as he was.

"Nothing that can't wait." The pair of curious song-birds turned their eyes in unison to the clasped hands, Turner's impatience more than enough to arouse question, let alone the picture of Honey linked to him by something that seemed more than a mere hand hold. They answered in a jumble of half-confused, half-embarrassed replies.

"We needed a hand with . . . with . . . something."

"No we didn't," Teresa interjected, giving Gerry a nudge. "We just wanted you to know we were going to take Indian and head on back to town, *weren't we Gerry?*"

"Ah . . . yeah."

"Indian's already taken Charlene back to town." Turner shot holes in their hastily fabricated excuses. "And that's not a bad idea. I've got some things that can't wait to be discussed. Why don't you meet us there?"

"Right." Honey saw her chance. "I'll go in with Teresa and Gerry and meet you there."

The hand tightened on hers, preventing the escape.

"You'll come with me." End of discussion.

Everyone else agreed, and was it by unspoken consent that she was left to drive back with Turner? She thought so. She was working in a nest of potential Cupids whose only fault was that they wanted to see her happy. What they failed to consider was that "happy" was a state of consciousness denied to her as long as the mines and all they had done to her life were there, like a specter over her head, and Turner was there, unwilling to exorcise them.

CHAPTER SEVEN

SEATED AROUND THE Caldwell dining room table, they finished the barbecue dinner Pauline had insisted she prepare, and waited for Turner to bring up the subject that had been on their minds for days. The problem was the same: a lack of time. What they waited to hear was Turner's solution to the problem.

As soon as the dishes were cleared he flipped his notebook open and studied it for a moment, as if staring at the facts would make some of them disappear, and chewed on the eraser of his pencil silently until everyone had quieted down.

"We have two thirds of the original number of mines left to investigate," he began. "And half the time we alloted for the whole has been spent. As I see it, we only have one or two options to go with since you can't work indefinitely and I have to turn in an opinion soon. We can make a decision as to the fate of the mines already checked, and leave the remainder of the mines, those farthest from town uninvestigated. Or we can find ways to maximize the time we have left and try to do them all."

"I don't like leaving a job half finished," Gerry declared adamantly. "I'm all for speeding things up if we can. And you know I'm not afraid of a little hard work."

"I want them all closed." Honey said her piece, not afraid of even a lot of very hard work if it meant the mines would be closed.

Teresa was more skeptical. "That's fine; we're all willing, but what we need is another eight hours in each day of the few days we have left. As it is, the only time we waste, if you can call it waste, is the time we spend going back and forth to the house and that we use in setting up in the morning and packing up at night. We can't eliminate any of that time unless we camp on the mine doorstep."

They all stopped in interested silence.

"Did I say that?" Teresa marveled at her own unintended ingenuity, the solution to their problems.

"It would be efficient," Gerry said.

"I think it would be fun," Teresa advocated her idea, voting her approval.

Turner tapped the pencil on the table, contemplating the thought. "It just might do the trick at that. We must use up . . . what . . . three hours a day in travel and set up time?"

"No, not that much." Honey put her opinion into the pot. "But we spend quite a bit and we'll surely spend more the farther we have to travel to reach the mines at the end of the park."

Charlene had, up until now, been content to sit back and sip a long cold gin and tonic, barely involved in the conversation or with the people at the table. Her ears perked up at this bit of information.

"I can't believe you're serious." She directed the criticism to Turner, treating the rest of them like so many pieces of unwanted furniture. "Have you gone one hundred percent cowboy on me, Turner Jameson? The man I came to meet here in this . . . this little backwater of a town is not the man I see before me. Sleep in a sleeping bag, on the ground, outside, with the sand and the snakes and . . ." She stood, speechless, unable or unwilling to take it farther with the man who not only was her boss but who was looking daggers at her.

"You don't understand." He directed the comment to her, intending it to be a silencer.

"No, I don't. Something has a hold on you here, something I think that's prejudiced your impartiality. At first you wanted to do all the mines because it would make the investigation complete and thorough. Now . . . now I've got to wonder if you aren't trying to stay here for other reasons, if you haven't already decided what your decision is, and are just gathering more evidence. Whose side are you on, Turner?"

Honey would have given a great deal to know the answer to that herself, but she wasn't to hear it from his lips. He sat, like the great stone face, neither confirming nor denying her suspicions.

"Are you coming with us to finish the job, or are you going to stay here and relay information to and from the home office?" It was as if she had never asked the questions.

Clearly Charlene did not want to come, but something told her that if she didn't, there might not be much of the Turner Jameson that she knew left when he returned. "I'll go." She tapped her foot, debating on her next move. "But if I have to suffer through sand fleas and tarantulas and no bathrooms and all the torments a desert survival team would have to put up with, you're going to have to make it worth my while. I want to take a last look at civilization before we all turn into hermits and make the trek into the unknown. I want to go into town for the evening, maybe take in a couple of shows."

The tension evaporated in the face of what everyone apparently thought was a good idea, no matter who the initiator of it was.

"It's only for a week, not a decade, but now that you mention it, I could do with a little R & R. How about you, Gerry?"

"Settled, as long as I don't have to go formal and as

long as you'll agree to keep me company."

Gerry asked for the date a lot more casually than
Honey suspected he felt, and she wondered if perhaps
the two would-be cupids hadn't caught each other in the
spell they'd meant for her and Turner.

Turner . . . her face warmed as she thought of him and
spending the evening with him . . . with them all, she
corrected herself. Teresa and Gerry would be there, of
course Charlene, and maybe Indian as well. Still. . . . She
mentally took note of her wardrobe in an effort to decide
what to wear. She didn't notice when the others left the
room, each to get ready for a long deserved night out.

"What are you puzzling about?" Turner remained on
the far side of the table, but he looked at her with such
an intimate intensity that if he had been seated right next
to her, he could hardly have seemed closer.

"Nothing much." She pushed her chair back and got
up to move around, slightly embarrassed to be caught
daydreaming. "It's too silly to mention."

"Nothing that makes you look like that is too silly to
mention. You remind me of a little girl at Christmas,
wondering which package she should open first."

"Actually, I was wondering what to wear tonight . . . something frilly and feminine, or something
daring and seductive . . ." Why had she admitted that?

It was enough encouragement for him to get up from
his far corner and come to where she stood. "As long
as it isn't black and gloomy, I'll enjoy seeing you in it."
He kissed the top of her hair lightly. "You'll come with
me?"

She did not answer at once, poised between a past
that would not give her up and a future that called out
to her appealingly. What was the big deal? It was a
date—and a casual date at that—not a marriage. Why
then did she feel that just one slip might wash all her
defenses away, like the waters of an immense lake trick-
ling through one small hole in a dam, little by little
until the barriers are eaten away and there is nothing left
to hold the water back.

"We'll have chaperones," he teased.

"Look at me." She shared the nervousness as if sharing it with him could make it commonplace and nothing special. "I haven't gone out with anyone in years. You'd think it was my first high school date."

"It is in a way." He rubbed a small area on her shoulders with his fingertips sending delightful shivers down her arms. "It's your first date with me, and it won't be like any other you've ever had. It means more, and I don't mind that you can't pretend it doesn't. I like the excitement I see in your face. I like knowing it's there for me. I like knowing I'm more to you than just a casual friend, because I've wanted more than that from you for such a long time and finally... finally you're giving me the chance to try and get it."

It was too much intimacy all at once. "The only thing you're going to get is recriminations if we're late getting dressed to meet the others. Why don't you go ahead, and I'll tell Pauline that we're going?"

"Did I hear my name mentioned?" Pauline chose that moment to come in from the kitchen, her starched apron still in place.

"Yes." Honey hesitated. Convincing her mother-in-law might prove even harder than convincing herself. "We... we all thought it would be nice if we could go into Las Vegas for the evening. We really need a break before this pilgrimage begins and there's a good show at the Sahara I've been wanting to see. It would be fun." Honey watched and listened to herself from the outside looking in, displeased with her method of handling the situation, yet unable to stop or change the monologue. It was as if she felt obligated to ask Pauline's permission.

"I'll be ready in a few minutes." Turner moved to leave them, but stopped near the stairs, waiting for Honey.

"You go ahead and enjoy yourself." Pauline treated him to a rare condescending smile as she drifted airily by to pull two chairs out from the diningroom table. "Honey and I will make some tea, play a little cards, and leave all the late-night socializing to you young couples. We'd prefer that, wouldn't we, dear?" In a world of her own making, Pauline was entirely convinced of her correct responses.

Turner left the stairs. "Honey enjoys her evenings with you, I know. But it's been a hard week or so for her, too, and I've asked her to come out with me tonight."

"But she doesn't ever do that. She never goes out at night," Pauline said.

"I know she hasn't in the past, but things change. She'll be going out with me tonight," he insisted firmly.

"Oh...on a date?" The tight smile remained fixed, but Pauline's expression had faded and her eyes held a remnant of the fear Honey had seen lurking in their depths every day since Daryl's accident. She could not be responsible for making that fear worse. It wasn't the time, and there would have to be a better way. "Oh, no, Mother," she stammered, as if that had been the farthest thing from her mind. "It's nothing like that. Turner didn't mean it that way precisely." She sent him an imploring glance. "We were *all* going out, not just Turner and I."

"Well, that's a relief." She held a hand over her heart and laughed shakily. "I should be ashamed of myself for carrying on so. Of course, Honey wouldn't *date*. She *can't* date."

The look Turner cast in Honey's direction was long and full of meaning. "No, I guess she can't. My apologies."

"Well then, now that that's settled, Honey, dear, why don't I just go get the cards while Turner and the others get ready to go?"

Honey found she couldn't look up or speak to Pauline, the pain a lump in her throat, the resentment a physical thing in her breast. But who did she resent? It couldn't be Pauline; the fault wasn't hers. She could feel the sting of tears threatening behind her eyelids. Tonight would be an evening exactly like almost every other one she had spent—like every one she had endured—since Daryl died. Before Turner, she hadn't found it confining, had even consciously preferred it to the invitations she received. She had preferred to spend her time alone, with only Pauline and her memories for companionship. But now.... Oh, now a thousand things were different, and he was the catalyst for them all, the reason for them all. She was living again. Why was that truth so painful to admit?

"Just because Daryl is dead, Honey, doesn't make it wrong for you to be alive." His anger had evaporated, transforming itself into something verging on pity, which was worse. She didn't want his pity.

"I want to believe that."

"And I want to convince you," he said through clenched teeth. "I *will* convince you! You aren't... you don't number among my lost causes yet!"

Pauline bustled into the dining area, a much used deck of cards in her hand. "Ready?"

Honey bit her full lower lip. She no longer wanted to bury herself with the past. She *wanted* to feel again, to live and to have a present and a future with more in it than gin rummy and empty bedrooms.

"Convince me. Don't give up on me." It was a wish, a prayer softly said, but unheard. Turner had gone, and Pauline had stopped listening a long time ago to anything but what she wanted to hear.

Honey was grateful for the flurry of activity the next morning, not wanting to lounge around the breakfast table discussing the night before. Undoubtedly they had had a good time. She had heard them come in, everyone evidently deciding to spend the night there and get an early start the next morning rather than scatter to their respective homes. She purposely waited until she heard the commotion of several voices before coming down to join them the next morning.

"Morning Teresa." She shouldered a sleeping bag and headed for the door with it, joining their human assembly line.

"Hi," a cheery voice answered her. "You should have

come with us last night. You..."

"Did you have a good time?" She wanted to get the first word in.

"Yes, but it would have been better if you'd been there."

"I was tired." She packed the bag into the Bronco, stuffing it into an oddly shaped corner left after the bulkier canned food had gone in.

"You must have been. You slept later than any of us. Turner wanted to wake you but Pauline said no."

Pauline again. "Do you know where he is?"

Teresa called back to her from the house. "Out in front talking to Pauline, I think. What's up with those two?"

"Never mind." She'd have enough trouble explaining why she had done what she had done last night to Turner, let alone having to explain it to Teresa, too. "I'll tell you later." Teresa had a thankfully short memory.

"Going somewhere?" Turner met her going around to the front of the house.

"Yes, I wanted to find you, to talk to you."

"You were headed the wrong way. I'm beginning to wonder if you'll ever be headed in the right direction." It didn't appear that the R & R had helped him much.

She put her arms around his neck boldly, squashing the niggling little uncertainties. "Am I headed in the right direction now?"

His features didn't soften, but he didn't make an effort to remove her hands from his body. "Honey, I have neither the time nor the patience, nor the inclination for games. You can't turn me on and you can't turn me off like a faucet as if we were high school kids caught petting under the bleachers at a basketball game every time Pauline comes around."

"If you'd only try to understand why I did it." She knew very well he referred to last night.

"It doesn't matter," he said flatly. "The time has come for you to make some decisions about your own life and what you want from it, without consulting Pauline or anyone else."

"My decision is to wait!" She glared at him. "Why do I have to do everything according to *your* time schedule? Why do I have to stuff the meeting and courtship and lovemaking that would normally take place over months or even years into a few weeks?"

"You don't," he said simply. "But I'm only here for a short while. I won't stay on with only empty promises to go on. I left as a boy because the promise of the land proved empty. I can't wait any longer for miracles to happen, no matter how much I might like to. Honey, I'm thirty-four years old and I feel like I've been waiting for you forever, certainly since the first time I saw your picture. How much longer do I have to put my feelings on hold?"

"You can't blame me because you gave up on the desert too soon, and you can't blame me if you cared for me and I didn't even know it."

"I can't blame you or myself if that happiness I always wanted to find out here isn't really here, if the promise of it was only a mirage I created because I wanted it so damned badly. But you also can't ask me to stay and delude myself for the rest of my life."

"So what you're saying is, make your decision now, because it's the last chance you'll have? How long are you giving me—ten minutes? Until the end of the week?"

They shouted at each other now, communication a painful and elusive thing. "How long would I have to wait unless I did set limits? Six months? A year? Two years? Ten? Or would I have to wait until Pauline dies too?"

She gasped, stilled into silence, and put a hand to her mouth. "How can you ask that? Do you know how horrible that sounds?"

"Yes!" he exploded. "The whole situation is appalling! Do you think I get some perverse satisfaction out of loving a woman who is in love with a ghost, who denies every honest physical and emotional response she has out of fear someone will see? Don't you understand?" He lowered his voice and drew her closer. "You make me feel as if I should apologize every time I touch you.

You make me feel like we're committing adultery every
time I kiss you." He shook his head. "I find myself
wanting you, and hating myself for wanting you at the
same time. And you, you want me just as much. It's
there for anyone with eyes to see, and yet you insist on
denying it to Pauline, though waiting isn't going to make
the telling any easier for you. But what's worse, you
deny it to yourself. I don't know how much longer I can
wait, trying to be platonic, for your sake or anyone
else's."

"I'm not asking you to wait or to stay." She didn't
want the responsibility of his feelings, of his very happiness placed on her shoulders. There were enough people expecting that of her already, and she wasn't sure she
could handle any of it.

"Are you asking me to go? Is that your decision then?
Do you want me out of your life for good?"

Her eyes slid up from his muscular legs, defined under
the tight Levi's, up from his broad chest clad in western
shirt, to rest on his face. There was a question there, an
expectation of pain, and a last look of desire of such
intensity that she could have melted like butter in its
heat. And that was her undoing, for seeing him that way
was like a mirror to her own feelings, and among other
things, it set her pulses to racing.

"No." She breathed the word. "I don't want you to
go. I don't know how I can arrange for you to stay, but
I don't want you to leave me."

"You're the best inducement for desert living I've
seen so far. If I were you, I'd talk to the Chamber of
Commerce about a job." Words failed him, and she felt
herself caught in his arms, any second thoughts she may
have had swept away by her first thoughts which were
only of him and the way he made her feel. There was
room for nothing else but the flash flood of emotion that
swept over her, and in that instant if he had asked her
to make love to him where they stood, hidden only by
the early morning shadows of the house, she would have
offered no objections. Hunger for him was a physical

ache deep within her, an empty need that demanded to be fulfilled.

Her thighs moved intimately against his, the primitive drives that held her captive not caring that she might wish she had used a modicum of discretion later. Time lost its meaning as she lost herself in his kiss, so new, so very unlike anything she had ever experienced before.

"God, it's a crime to let you go," he moaned huskily, ensnared in the same web of need as she. "But anyone seeing us would know. There would be no other way to explain this as other than what it is. And if you want to explain things diplomatically..."

"Hmmmmm." Intelligent response failed her at that moment, though she could see, could feel what he meant. One of his legs stood firmly planted between hers, her hips molded to his, his chest pressed to the material of her blouse. If not for the clothing that separated them, there would have been no separation at all.

"If I had an ounce of sense, I would take you here and now while I know you could be mine so easily."

"You're too much of a gentleman for that." She moved silkily against him, delighting in the long unused power of her womanhood.

"If I were you," he growled warningly, "I wouldn't count on that veneer of civilization too much. It's mighty thin at this point." He released her with shaking, reluctant fingers. "Come on. We'd better find some chaperones before I change my mind."

She followed him to where everyone waited, packing the last of the equipment into heavily laden vehicles.

"You're all ready to leave now?" Pauline came from the house to see them off. It looked as if she might have been crying. "I can't convince you to stay behind? You don't think they can take care of what needs doing without you?" She directed the plea and another of her piteous looks to Honey.

"No." If she was to stand up to her mother-in-law, it would have to be in little ways first. "It's going to take all six of us to do the job."

* * *

At the end of the first day, Honey wished they could have found twelve more volunteers to help. At the end of the second day she almost wished she'd followed Pauline's advice to stay home. Everyone had worked furiously, but there was still a lot more to do. Turner Jameson was very thorough, an admirable trait no doubt valued by his employers—and his lovers, the thought came along with the other—but at the moment, she wished he would consider being just a bit less efficient. She slumped down in the shade of the Bronco to rest, unseen for a moment.

"I refuse to work another minute today, another second, Turner Jameson, so don't even suggest it," she warned him as he found and approached her. "Even God rested on the seventh day! I'm tired and I'm dirty and I'm tired of getting dirty in the mines. Come to think of it, I'm sick of the mines, of crawling around like a horny toad under ground and..."

"I get the message, and not only from you." He looked over his shoulder to the column of sand-covered people who trudged from the latest opening in the earth, ancient trolls come to wreak havoc on the above-ground dwellers. Teresa was first.

"You are a slave driver." She spoke to Turner pointedly before filing the samples she carried in a box and sitting down next to Honey to transcribe her notes.

"Gold mine; one main shaft; twenty feet in. Floor angles sharply downward; timbers weak." She stopped scribbling, formulating her notes aloud. "Indian, do you have the exact figures on those tunnel supports? I want to include everything in this one package."

"Speaking of packages..." Gerry removed his gloves and rubbed his hands together. "What's in our packages for dinner? I'm starved."

Charlene wiped at her face with a premoistened towelette and inspected the contents of yet another box, lifting vacuum packed bags up and setting them down with an equal lack of interest. "Does it matter?" she asked sarcastically. "It all tastes the same. Uggh. I refuse to eat this garbage for another night."

"For once we agree." Indian handed the information she'd sought to Teresa and dropped his portion of the samples in along with the rest. He then slung a light backpack of his personal possessions over his shoulder and turned his back on the camp, setting out overland. "I'll be back with dinner."

"I'll take an order of fried chicken," Charlene called after him in annoyance. She dropped her arms in despair when he didn't answer. "Honestly, where does he think he's going to get food out there?" she asked no one in particular. "The only thing there is to eat is what we have here in camp."

Honey, Gerry, and Teresa smiled to themselves, even more so when Indian returned, as they had known he would, less than an hour later with three jack rabbits hung from his belt.

"Dinner." He issued the smug pronouncement while skinning the rabbits and preparing to roast them over the open fire, aided by Turner who surprisingly picked up the skill rather quickly.

But in contrast to Indian's delight, shared by the other native enthusiasts, Charlene had turned pale, her gaze caught and held on the rabbits in repugnant fascination.

"The nearest I've ever come to rabbit is when I used to wear a cheap winter coat. You aren't seriously going to eat that?" The rest of them were already beyond salvation, but she couldn't believe that Turner would.

"Why not?"

"It's kind of like strong chicken." Gerry turned one of the smallest pieces of meat, skewered on sticks over the coals, so that the other side browned. "You've got to try some."

"I'd sooner eat rattlesnake," she exclaimed facetiously.

"That's not bad either," Teresa recalled. "Though you have to cook it right." She related her story to the others.

"I remember the first time I ever cooked one. I coiled it, uncut, in a frying pan and turned on the heat. The crazy thing, coiled tighter and tried to strike at me, headless, mind you. Scared me out of my wits."

There was laughter all around, save for Charlene whose pale complexion was tinged now with green.

"Tasty stuff, rattlesnake, if you prepare it right. Rabbit's better though." Teresa stole Gerry's small piece of meat. "Are you sure you don't want any, Charlene? Honestly, it's good." She licked her fingers. "Turner, did you have the foresight to pack any barbecue sauce?"

"That's Honey's department, not mine." He snatched a piece of rabbit from the flames too, juggling it, hot potato-like, between his hands until it had cooled enough to eat.

"Please, let's go back to town." Charlene had reached the end of her frayed and tightly stretched nerve. "I haven't had a bath in three days, or brushed my teeth properly, and my hips are sore from sleeping on the ground, and my skin is peeling. I can't eat... any of that. Turner, you've seen enough. Surely you've seen enough?"

He leaned back in the lawn chair, pulled up close to the fire, and looked at the fading sunset beyond Charlene. "No, I haven't. I've been away for fifteen years. It's going to take longer than I've been here so far to see... enough."

"One must be careful," Indian warned him prophetically. "By the time one sees enough of this desert, one has sometimes seen too much to want to leave."

"This isn't a vacation, Turner. Or had you forgotten? Or a trip down memory lane. We're on assignment, remember?"

"These are my off hours, Charlene." His mouth moved almost without sound, and, had the evening not been so still, Honey doubted any but Charlene would have heard. "What I do with them is of no concern to anyone but myself, not to the government... not to you. Is that clear?"

"Fine." Her eyes blazed angrily at him. "What I do with my off hours isn't regulated either then, and I refuse to spend one more second of them here." She added meaningfully, "I think what I will do is go back to town and do my best to hurry this investigation up a bit before you lose what small amount of perspective you have left!"

He watched her climb into one of their three vehicles and leave, but he didn't make a move to follow. The conversation stopped short, then resumed with an abnormal, stilted quality until they realized Charlene's leaving, and her threats had not had the negative effect on Turner that they might have had several weeks ago. If anything, he was even more relaxed in her absence, rolling his sleeves up with the rest of them to partake of the remainder of the rabbits and dehydrated side dishes they'd prepared to go along with the game.

They squatted around the fireside in preference to the spindly card table originally set up for that purpose, and ate the juicy rabbit with their fingers, scooping up dehydrated vegetables from a common bowl with plastic spoons reminding Honey of her girl scout days. Turner had come a long way. Finally, the meal over, they relaxed against the bedrolls while Honey poured coffee from a metal pot that had been simmering on a flat rock next to the coals. Turner let out a more than satisfied sigh and pulled her down beside him when she'd replaced the pot. It was a comfortable, friendly embrace, full of warmth and companionship and without the sexual overtones that usually sparked between them when contact was made, and she settled against his chest easily, letting her head come to rest on his shoulder without reservation.

"You know, in Reno or Las Vegas you can't see the night sky like you can here." He pointed out a constellation to her. "The lights from the casinos, the streetlights, the airports . . . it all drowns out the starlight. Even the moon looks different out here."

"Seen from a different perspective," Indian interjected lazily.

She liked the way in which they said "different." "It has always been different here... special. Coming from somewhere else, as I do, it was easy to see. People who've lived here all their lives don't appreciate it in the same way that someone coming from somewhere else can."

"I sometimes wonder why I left." Turner tightened his hold on her.

"Job prospects," Gerry prompted. "That's why most of us leave."

"If it weren't for the gift shop," Teresa agreed. "I would have had to leave a long time ago. But that doesn't explain why you haven't come back, Turner. I mean, you have job security now, you could transfer or commute couldn't you?"

"Stop it," Honey commanded. "You're acting like a couple of evangelists. I'm sure Turner can weigh the pros and cons of where he should live without us trying to convert him."

"It's a matter of choice," Indian pointed out to them. "You don't like the city, so you think he shouldn't like it, too. He must like it, or he wouldn't stay. No one lives forever the life he... or she... does not like. One weighs what is really important against what only seems important. This life is not for everyone."

Turner stretched and stood with his back against the fire, staring out in the direction of the city he had left behind. "It's not always that easy. Sometimes the choices aren't yours alone to make. It depends upon so many things."

She longed to ask him what things prevented him from coming back; or even if he wanted to come back. Was it Charlene who seemed to have a hold over him, if only in his business world? Was it she who made him hang on to one life, while embracing another? Was he torn between one course of action and it's direct opposite just as Honey herself was?

She longed to ask him, she needed to ask him before she could make any decisions of her own. But Gerry had

added more wood to the fire, and thus more light, and
Teresa had picked up her battered guitar for a round of
lively music, and no one was inclined to sleep or leave
them in the privacy she wanted.

She turned her head away from him to look into the
fire. Love, if that was what she felt growing within her,
was much more complicated a thing the second time
around.

CHAPTER EIGHT

HONEY'S BROWS PUCKERED together in confusion. What could Charlene be doing? Why hadn't she come back? They took fewer breaks and shorter ones and still accomplished more without Charlene present. And everyone but Turner breathed easier. Only he kept a worried eye tuned toward Pahrump. It was easy to see who he was thinking about.

Indian broached the subject that had occupied both her and, much to her consternation, Turner's thoughts all day. "How will she find us if she wants to return to work?"

"She won't come back to work," Turner assured him. "When, not if, she comes back, she'll probably be bringing people with her, but it won't be to work. In any case, we're not all that hard to find. Pauline has our itinerary, and I have a feeling she'll be only too glad to show Charlene the way. And, there's always the radio."

Indian shook his head. "We'll be out of radio range by tomorrow because of the mountains and the distance."

"They'll probably locate us before then." He handed Indian the schedule which Honey peered at in half interest over his shoulder. She hadn't seen a complete list of all the mines to be investigated. It hadn't been important since all of them should be looked into. That was her goal. She only looked now because Turner had intimated the investigation might be somehow disrupted, and she wanted to see which mines were left that might be overlooked.

Her breath caught sharply at one of the mines, only a dozen or so from the end of their long list, and only a few from the one they were gathering samples from now. The Silver Dollar Lady mine had been so named by a gentleman from Virginia City, Nevada, who'd come to the Pahrump area in search of silver. He claimed to have been guided to the right spot to dig one night after consuming a quart of whiskey, guided there by a lady dressed in a long gown made entirely of silver dollars. The mine had proven itself lucky for him. It hadn't been as lucky for Daryl who shared the bottom of the shaft with the man he'd gone to rescue. There had been no safe way to bring them up after the cave-in and no one, including herself, wanted to risk the living. But, oh, how hard it had been to close that mine, to seal it forever. She clenched her teeth together, trying to focus her thoughts elsewhere before the ones that crowded her mind now overwhelmed her. She snatched a pen from the clipboard and, much to Indian's surprise, inked out the Silver Dollar Lady.

"No need to do this one," she said flippantly. "I happen to know it's well sealed. A cave-in filled the shaft." That and a lot of dynamite had finished the job, but she didn't add that. Indian would know, but Turner wouldn't and she couldn't speak of it rationally yet.

"Don't tell him, Indian," she asked when Turner went back to check on the others' progress.

"The only secrets I tell are my own."

The others kept their silence as well, waiting for her to speak, thunder clouds on the horizon, threatening her peace of mind with their dark, meaningful looks, looks that became more questioning and came more often as the other mines before the Silver Dollar Lady were done. When there was only the Lady left, she avoided them entirely, preferring Turner's ignorance to their knowledge.

She rode in the Bronco with him, content to let him drive them both down the dirt track she knew so well, whose every curve and corner were etched in indelible ink into her brain. Weary, he didn't notice her growing agitation, or the fact that she could not speak for the lump in her throat, and she was grateful for that. Her emotions were too raw. Perhaps Pauline had been right, perhaps coming back here for the first time, after all this time, was a mistake. The site was as she remembered it. Funny how well preserved the desert kept some things, like the pad that had been cleared eighteen months ago for the helicopter bringing in officials and the first emergency crews. If one was needed in this same spot today, the same pad could be used. There were no tire tracks there to indicate anyone had ever been there, but there were other telltale signs. The vegetation that they had trampled over in their haste had not yet grown back. There was no life at all in front of the mine that had once been there.

She got out of the Bronco in a semidaze, aware that Teresa, Gerry, and Indian followed the familiar road too, somewhere behind them, and that Turner was right behind her, surveying this as he had all the rest. Couldn't he sense a difference?

She scooped up a handful of the rock that made up this low hill and the mine underneath. The dynamite had shattered it like so much fragile glass; the cave-in had done the same, turning it into sand. She let the material trickle from her hand. Odd. It had seemed so solid before when she had entered with Daryl to yell encouragements to the man they were to rescue from the shaft. It had seemed to be so stable when Daryl drilled into it and hooked up a safety line. Rock hard. Wasn't that what people said? People were wrong. She had been wrong, so wrong to trust in a strength that had been only an illusion . . . only a mirage. It was a term Turner had used, a desert term and quite, quite appropriate. She dropped the earth from her hand entirely as if it stung her palm, and swayed, for a moment losing her balance as the memories assaulted her, inflicting a nearly physical pain.

Turner caught her against him, supporting her with his arms, and for a second she considered throwing herself into his arms and pouring out all the hurt and frustration and anger Daryl had left there, locked up inside.

She rubbed her hands against the fabric of his shirt sleeves. Now was not the time or the place to tell him. Certainly she couldn't hope to speak of it dispassionately and if she broke down, would he think she had engineered it all to convince him of her point of view? And what if that cold, uncaring man Charlene had brought with her from Reno returned to replace the warm, understanding man she sensed he was becoming? He acted so strong, so reliable now . . . like the rock in the mine. But was he? Could she count on him to support and back her when she needed it most, when the anger was brought back to her afresh just by seeing the mine? Could she count on him to help her bury the past when to do so might violate his own code of impartially fair ethics? She could not take the risk. The feeling between them was too fragile.

"Is Honey all right?" Gerry alighted from the Jeep on the run.

"I was just about to ask her that myself. I think it's just too much work in one day out in the sun," Turner diagnosed, confident that he knew her state of mind. "Let's camp here for the night. It's late and we can investigate this one tomorrow."

"No, let's not." Gerry spoke quickly, stopping his runaway tongue in time to prevent spilling the beans entirely, which clearly he would have liked to do.

"Why not?" Turner demanded, his eyes on Honey's pale face. "She's dead on her feet. I say it's time to call it quits." He marched off to set up camp, leaving her to face a bewildered Gerry. "Why in heaven's name haven't you told him?" he demanded.

How could she explain? "I don't know really. I suppose if I told him and his reaction was too casual, I'd be angry. And I couldn't bear it if he were the reverse ... grief stricken. This place has brought so much unhappiness to so many." She tried to piece the jigsaw puzzle of reasons around into some kind of workable order and gave up. "Wouldn't it be better if he could treat this like any of the other mines?" She paced back and forth in a short space in front of the hill. "Don't you see, I can block some of the feeling this way. I can hide how it makes me feel because I *have* to. If he knew, if he looked at me the same way the rest of you have since this afternoon, like you expected me to break. Gerry ..." She faltered. "I just might break. I really might. And I've come so close to forgetting!"

"No you haven't. You can't forget something you've never faced. You haven't faced anything. You've hidden it away and promised yourself that you won't look at it, and now you're asking the rest of us to go along with the pretense. We're worried about you." He took one of her trembling hands and held it tightly. "We want to help you if we can, and neither Teresa nor I feel spending the night here is going to do that." He looked over his shoulder to see if Turner was returning. "But the only way to convince him to leave is to tell him the truth."

"No! Please!"

"Don't you think you owe it to him?" He tried another tactic. "To let him see all sides of you is what love is all about."

"I don't love him!" She looked at the mine. "How can you say that here? Now?"

"What would be the difference if I said it yesterday or tomorrow or anywhere else? How long can you hide it? All of us can see how you feel."

"What did you do, rehearse this together? You've learned the same lines!" It wasn't fair to attack Gerry, but it came out that way.

"Well you haven't learned them at all." Teresa joined

them, blunt as usual. "I'm telling you this is no way to conduct a love affair."

"It isn't love . . . and it isn't an affair."

"That kiss in paradise the other day was . . . brotherly?" Teresa didn't play by any rules. She made it a point to hit below the belt. "The only reason you haven't had an affair is that no one's left you alone long enough." She caught a glimpse of Turner's approaching figure out of the corner of her eye. "But if that's the way you want to run things, okay. Gerry and I will stay out of it."

"We will?" He raised an eyebrow at her.

"What is this?" Turner demanded, hands on hips. "Is this Nevada's version of the Bermuda Triangle? You don't want to stay here. Indian's flatly refused to. Something about unhappy ground." He kicked at the soil with his boot and looked at Honey skeptically. "It looks in sad shape, but nothing that a little water and manure wouldn't cure, and it looks a damn sight better than the land I own does—and I even have hopes for that someday."

She laughed and linked her arm through his, pulling him away from the mine and back to the camp he had set up for them some distance away. She was glad she hadn't told him, glad to see the humor in his face where she saw pity in everyone else's. If she was to put the past behind her, it was not by resurrecting the past and laying it out to look at all over again; she could only hope to replace the bad memories, the negative associations with happier ones.

"I think Indian just wants to eat the rabbits he's probably out to catch all by himself this time, and leave us with dried tuna casserole and banana chips because we made such pigs of ourselves last time."

"Probably," he moaned. "I'm beginning to wish I'd put in a food order to go with Charlene before she left. She should be turning up any time now and I could use her fried chicken."

They busied themselves around the camp, Gerry and Teresa like nervous canaries around an unpredictable cat;

Honey ignoring them and their surroundings as much as she could. It didn't help to dwell on it and she was sick of sadness that got in the way of her happiness.

And if the meal was tasteless to her palate, still she ate every morsel, downing it with a much hoarded bottle of rosé, and even produced a bag of miniature marshmallows for dessert afterwards.

Turner threw another piece of wood onto the fire and put on a light jacket against the night cold before sitting down so close as to be all but on top of her. "You look warm. How do you do it, take the temperature swings so readily?"

"I'm warm blooded." She smiled and handed him the bag of marshmallows and a coil of stiff wire. He cut a piece from it and began to string the marshmallows onto its length, working diligently for a while in silence.

"Do you know how many of these things I've strung on here? Forty-six." He answered the rhetorical question. "And I'm not through yet. A man could die of hunger just getting enough on here to cook."

"Not if the man keeps eating them as fast as you've been eating these before they even get to the fire."

He chewed guiltily and finished the string, holding it over the flames casually, turning it over and over to toast on all sides.

"Where did Gerry and Teresa get off to?"

Honey hadn't noticed that they weren't there. She shrugged unconcerned. "For a walk?"

"At this time of night, after the day we put in? No, if they're walking, it's only until they're out of sight. I strongly suspect that I may have a rival for Teresa's full attention. What do you think?"

"I'd say you were right about their motives. You're losing admirers right and left." She was thinking of Charlene's abrupt departure.

Turner tuned in to the thought. "Charlene was never my type. Not that we never had a social relationship outside the office; we did, but not of a permanent variety for either of us. She's much more interested in her career than she will ever be in one particular man, unless he can offer her a business advantage."

"That's terrible." If it was an example of the new morality, she wanted no part in it.

"Not really. She places value on other things. Anyway, it doesn't matter...she doesn't matter. I suppose what I was trying in my roundabout way to tell you is that you have no competition."

She shied away from the implication. "You say that now. Wait until Theresa smells the aroma of marshmallows. Love her dearly as I do, I don't think Gerry stands a chance if you have the food. Like moths to a flame. I've never seen anyone consume marshmallows like Teresa. Speaking of which, yours are burning."

He blew fire from the end and popped a piece of the melting confection into his mouth.

"Good?"

"Mmmmmm," he mumbled. "Hard to tell with a mouth full of seared tongue. Want a taste?"

"Why not?" She reached for the shish-ka-bobbed spun sugar but he held it out of her reach and offered his lips instead, taking it as an acceptance when she didn't move, parting her lips with his tongue. It was a thoroughly deep and decidedly sweet kiss.

"Well?" He paused for a moment and she licked her mouth, slowly taking in the taste of both him and the candy.

"I've had marshmallows before, but there's a difference here. They say everything tastes better if it's cooked over an open campfire. Do you think that's it?"

He bent over her again, the firelight turning her honey blond hair a rich, warm auburn. He drank in her appearance thirstily. "I've been roasting over an open fire since I first saw you. You're like a flame from top to bottom."

"I'm a country girl. Is that a compliment?"

"Yes," he mumbled, deliciously nibbling at her neck, leaving sticky but somehow satisfying trails of marshmallow residue in his tongue's wake. "I tell you that I'm on fire for you, and you ask if that's a compliment. I half think that's what has Charlene piqued. She thought she'd found a kindred soul in me. I'm not normally an emotional, demonstrative man, at least I wasn't for years. My career, my work was all there was for me . . . and for her, too, in a way. Perhaps we convinced ourselves that we didn't need any more, that we didn't want any more. But lately I haven't been a shining example of cool uninvolvement. My needs are different than before, and I can think of only one positive thing just now to go back to the city for."

"And what's that?" She didn't really care. It was a way to make conversation, to listen to his talk, to hear his voice and add another sensation to the ones he was already assaulting her with.

"Well, to put it bluntly it isn't as though we have a room where we can put a 'do not disturb' sign on the door."

"You're assuming an awful lot, don't you think?" She *didn't* think so, and she doubted he thought so either, but it was something to say, a part of the game she played at.

"You can stop this any time you want to. I'm assuming nothing, taking nothing for granted." Just the same, he lowered her back against the sleeping bag, his hand at the small of her back, bringing her hips up to meet his at his command. The sensation was delightfully sinful and warm, their bodies so close to the fire, and somewhere along the line it occurred to her that this was no longer a game, that she didn't want him to take his warmth away. She moaned softly in regret when he did so, the sound mellowing into a sigh when all he did was remove his jacket to place it under her head, resuming his exploration of her body. He drew in a deep breath when she responded to his lovemaking and returned it, tentatively at first, testing the temperature of her own feelings before letting herself go.

She fingered the hair at the base of his neck and pulled him closer, their eyes locked in understanding as she raised her head to meet his parted lips again half way.

"I want you." He said it unnecessarily, breathing the words onto her face.

She knew that he did, could feel his desire as he lay over her, could feel it in the way his hands trembled as they brushed the surface of her breasts uncertainly, a contact that became bolder as he felt her nipples harden to stiff points of desire at his touch.

"And I want you." She arched her back to increase the contact, caught up in the momentum of her own needs, the movement of her body decidedly sensual and intent.

He brushed the material of her blouse out of the way, and all thought left her save the thought of having him closer, his expertise banishing every other thought from her consciousness. She tilted her hips to give his hands better access to the zipper of her denims, urging him to hurry and be done with the clothing that separated them, urging him with low half whispered entreaties that only further enflamed him. She reached for him, touching him in half-shy, part wanton anticipation, wanting only to shed the last remaining inhibitions that held them apart, like so many layers of unwanted clothing.

"Turner..." She drew out the last syllable of his name, adding a wealth of meaning to the word, asking in the only way she could for what she knew was to follow. No. This was no game. Her body writhed in expectation as his hands held her hips in position, and still he waited.

"I've wanted this for so long. I've waited for this for so long." There was a shadow of...was it fear or regret in his voice?

She could not tell. But she laughed, a low throaty sound that was somehow in keeping with her mood. "Then what are you *waiting* for?" She stroked his arms with her hands, bringing them up to caress his shoulders and pull him down.

"I want to make love to you, not just have sex with you." His eyes fairly glowed with his intensity. "I have

to know something now, bad timing though it is...I
have to know!"

"Tell me." She feared losing the moment as well, an
unformed worry lurking in the back of her mind.

He closed his eyes, wanting to hear, but not quite sure
he wanted to see in her face the answer to his question.
"I'm not a drug to be taken to forget. I'm not a diversion
to replace...Damn it, Honey, I want to know who
you're making love to tonight! Is it me or is it just your
way of trying to forget him?"

He knew. Honey bolted away from him and his
odious, ill-timed, unanswerable questions. He
knew...and she had forgotten for a blessed moment just
where she was, who she was with, and who she was not
with.... In his arms she had forgotten it all, had wanted
to. Was there something so terribly wrong in that?

"Where are you going?" he demanded, as if he had
a right to demand anything of her after what he had just
done.

"Leave me alone." She dressed quickly and hugged
herself with shaking arms, her tears an empty gesture
now, mocking all that she had thought she stood for.

The night was cold, the wind brisk, but she welcomed
it and strode off alone, leaving the faint glow of the fire
and his still naked silhouette in the distance, in favor of
the chill of the mountain ahead of her. It was a chill that
no fire could warm, a loneliness without voice to re-
proach her. Ahead was only nothing, a cold, deep, sterile
void, an emptiness that was more heart rending than any
angry accusation could have been.

"Daryl!" She cried out his name, wanting to feel his
being, feel his anger or his censure. But there was nothing
there, only the mountain and the filled mine shaft beneath
it, and the emptiness she felt above it.

She slid to the ground, feeling the gritty grains of
gravel bite into her flesh, and, huddling next to an un-
forgiving earth, wept.

CHAPTER NINE

"Honey?"

There it came again, closer this time. She'd been
playing a subliminal game of hide and seek with the
various voices who called her name all night, hearing
them come closer then fade away and come close once
more, knowing all the time that as long as she didn't
want to be found and did not move or respond to the
voices, they would not find her. It was still pitch dark,
though only an hour or so from dawn, and she still could
not be seen. The only reason Teresa located her at all
was that it *was* so dark and the girl literally toppled over
her.

"Jesus, Mary, and Joseph!" Teresa hyperventilated
several times and jumped back to assure herself that
whatever or whoever she'd tumbled over was harmless.

"Honey? Honey, answer me. Is that you?" she demanded. "You've pulled a lot of crazy stunts in your
time, and there've been quite a few instances, especially
lately in which I've questioned your better judgment, but

I've never had occasion to doubt your sanity until tonight . . . correction . . . this morning. What in the
world happened to you and where have you been?"

She started to explain, knowing beforehand that it
would be a woefully inadequate and garbled explanation.
"I've been walking around the Silver Dollar Lady; I might
have dozed off for awhile. I needed to think and I knew
I wouldn't be able to do it with all of you clamoring at
me. I suppose I should have answered you, when I knew
it was you, but I thought *he* might still be around and I
didn't want to see him just yet."

"He, if you mean that emotional wreck of a man who
insisted we go out in the middle of the night to find you,
after I assured him you weren't lost, that you were probably just taking another of your nocturnal walks . . . *he*
left for town hours ago."

"For town?" Honey echoed.

"Yes, and there's some kind of trouble in town. Everyone's there except you and me, so if you're quite through
with your meditations, can we go? Gerry's waiting for
us in town!"

Honey put aside her personal problems for a moment.
"What's going on?"

"I wouldn't know," Teresa growled, not bothering to
pull her punches. "Some time after Turner left, we get
this frantic phone call from Pauline. She got a call from
someone else who got a call from someone else . . . you
know how it is . . . and the next thing I know, Gerry
orders me to find you and follow a.s.a.p. He and Indian
took off just a few minutes ago, so if we hurry, we might
be able to catch them."

They piled into Teresa's Jeep not bothering to pack
anything correctly, or in any order, just throwing it in
topsy-turvy until the camp was bare, the campfire now
sand covered smouldering out the only sign anyone had
been there.

"I can't think what Pauline's problem might be."
Honey shook her head in bewilderment. "Though it ap-
pears she isn't the only one to think it's a problem. As

to Turner and me, no mystery there. It's all very simple..." Nevertheless, she didn't think the explanation would get any easier with a dress rehearsal.

"Oh?" Teresa fished into her jacket pocket, keeping her eyes on the road ahead, and pulled out Honey's bra and socks. She handed them over, waiting expectantly. "I thought you might want these. You left them on Turner's sleeping bag intermingled with his clothes. I'd love to hear the *simple* explanation for this one, Honey."

"He asked me a question." It was a relief to speak of it to someone other than herself. Talking to herself half the night about it hadn't done her a bit of good. "He asked if I was making love to him to forget Daryl. He made it sound like I was using him, that I didn't care about him as a person. That he was only my means to the end... the end being temporary forgetfulness."

"He thinks that's what you were doing?" Teresa asked incredulously. "He doesn't know you very well. *You* don't think that's what you were doing?"

"No." The answers, some of the answers had come to her. "I left before anything happened. I left, not because I didn't care enough for him. I left because I care for him too much already, and I was scared to death that he might have been right, that if we had made love, I *would* have succeeded in forgetting Daryl." She covered her eyes with hands that didn't want to let her see the truth. "Life was so unfair to him, Terri..." She used her friend's pet nick name. "I feel like a Judas for loving someone other than him, and I feel guilty as hell for trying to open a fresh chapter in the book of my life until I've closed the mines and closed the old chapter. I made Daryl a promise, and I can't put him in the past until I've fulfilled it." She clenched her hands together in uncertainty. "I'm not sure, I'm just not sure..." She bent her head.

"Well I'm sure of a few things," Teresa began confidently. "I'm sure you've had too long a night to think about it any more. Let's get this business in town over and done with, whatever it is, and get back to work.

Work's a cure-all, and besides, from the looks of Turner last night, he can't handle many more delays in starting his portion of the book of your life. Don't worry, don't worry about that now. Worry about my driving instead."

The Jeep shot forward, traveling over the rough ground like a dune buggy, rarely with all four wheels on the ground at the same time, forcing Honey to hang on for dear life and think only of the next bump in the road until they arrived on the outskirts of town. Here Teresa slowed down to a modest 55, the official speed limit, to look around.

Most of the buildings were still closed, there being a few minutes until their usual opening time; the mostly deserted streets reflected that, yet even if the streets had been crowded, they would have noticed what Pauline's frantic problem must be by its very grandiose nature. The road leading to the country club where they were supposed to meet Gerry and the others was literally double parked with all sorts of heavy equipment, behemoth bull dozers next to huge back hoes next to colossal road graders next to massive trucks, all with tires that were larger then Teresa's Jeep as it cautiously crept by. She turned down the country club lane and pulled up into its parking lot, entering the coffee shop/casino that was open all night, looking for answers to the obvious question, answers that Honey feared she knew already.

Teresa spotted them at a table near the middle of the room, a table surrounded by large blue collar workers, making the area look like a union hall, dressed as the men were in hard hats, work clothes, and heavy steel-toed boots.

"Sorry we're late," Honey apologized before anyone had time to comment on it. "We saw all the equipment. Did the country club, on the spur of the moment decide to add another fifty rooms?" She knew that wasn't the answer; she knew what the answer was before anyone said what it was.

Gerry drummed his fingers on the table top help-lessly. "Someone called Reno and arranged for work to begin on the park at once. These fellows arrived last night."

Tension hung in the air like oppressive humidity, but Honey brought a chair from another table for Teresa and pulled one out for herself. They were in this together, weren't they?

The men did not introduce themselves, or sit down, but spoke directly to Turner. "So you'll have maps and a set of instructions for us to work from today?"

"Yes, I will." Turner stood and shook the man's hand on it. "You'll have them by nine A.M. I'm sure my associate, Ms. Mercer, whom I believe you met yesterday will have something worked out. I'll check it out and get back to you."

"Good enough." The men left.

Turner slumped back into his seat and poured a cup of coffee from the decanter on the table. He looked like he had been up all night, his cheeks stubbled with a day's growth of beard, his hair combed, but not with his usual care, his clothing rumpled, the same clothing he had worn last evening.

"Does anyone want to tell us what's going on here?" Honey looked from face to face; none of them except Indian would return her look. "Those men can't start breaking ground. We haven't finished the investigation yet."

"We *have* finished the investigation," Turner stated without preamble. "I'm sorry, but that's the way it is."

No explanation, not even a true apology, just another dictate. "I don't understand. Yesterday we were all set to finish the dozen or so mines left on the list. We were to be done in a few days. What happened between then and now to change your mind?" She could only think of one thing, but surely he wouldn't abandon the investigation because she had abandoned his bed? "Why can't you simply tell those men they can't start work until we're finished and your recommendation is turned in?" She had to press the point; no one else was.

"I can't do that." His voice was flat and tired. "For

one thing, the government pays the men the same wage whether they sit or work. It's all contracted for. I'm not responsible for them being here. I'm sorry that they are, but now that they are here, I can't justify not putting them to work or sending them away... even if I had the power to send them away. I no longer have that power."

"And to hell if the park they construct isn't safe for the people who use it, is that right?"

"Honey, you don't know the whole story," Gerry advised her. "I don't like it either, but it isn't his fault. He's been on the phone to the home office all morning. They've granted him certain concessions that are in our favor. They've agreed to automatically close any mines that are in the way of projected roads or hiking trails or buildings or designated camp sites."

"You must look at it as a victory for us." Indian treated her as he might a fragile flower, speaking quietly and convincingly. "Almost all of the mines will be filled in, to harm no one ever again, when the operating crews build the roads, cut the trails, grade the land, and level pads."

"It will be a part of the same job, you're saying?" Teresa asked them. "Are you saying we won't have to prove them unsafe, per se?"

"Yes, and those mines we've already seen to will be taken under consideration as well, based upon the facts we've been able to gather."

The others seemed to be taking what Honey saw as a large snag, if not an outright defeat, in their stride, pleased that Turner had done what he *had* done, not overly worried about what he had not done. She was the only one among them not satisfied with his pat answers, the only one who had expected more than miracles from the beginning.

"What about the mines we haven't seen to? What about your promise to investigate all the mines?"

"I can't keep it, Honey." Surely the defeat she saw in his face could not equal the disappointment that knifed through her.

"So we leave a dozen deathtraps out there, within walking distance to the new hiking trails you'll be building? Did you decide to leave just enough of them to give the S & R something to do when the park opens, or is this your...impersonal...objective method of revenge?"

"Honey!" Even Teresa was shocked at her friend's attitude, and she knew more than any of them did about its reasons.

"I'm not God, Honey." He swore softly, his hand clenched around the coffee cup so tightly she thought it might break from the pressure. "What do you want me to do, go out there and fill them all in by hand? Because that's the only way I can fill them in now. I've been pulled off this assignment permanently." He laid the facts out as they were. "Charlene has been placed in charge. She's the one who, in anticipation of her command, called the workers in, she's the one who will be presenting all the mine data to our superiors, and she's the one who is responsible for making the decisions concerning their closure. And finally, *she's* the one you need to lobby. Not me. I can't help you any more!"

"Any more?" She called after him as he left their table in favor of the bar. "Any help you ever gave us was taken forcibly. You just don't give a damn!" She wasn't sure why she followed him, no one else did, apparently wanting to give the two of them time and distance to air their problems privately. "So Charlene's behind all this. I should have known." She continued speaking to him though he had not acknowledged her presence. "What did she do, what could she possibly have done to convince them to pull you off this assignment if you hadn't asked to be relieved?"

"She told them the truth. She told them she thought I was becoming too emotionally involved in this issue. And she told them something they may not have known—that I used to live here and still own land here and that one of the people killed in the mines was my close friend."

"And they took her word over yours? They didn't give you a chance to defend yourself?" That sounded more than unfair, especially since Turner *had* been objective in the face of all temptation, painfully so as far as she was concerned. She had never really believed that he had abandoned the investigation because she had left him last night. It was too much out of character.

"They gave me a chance. They spoke to me about her concerns, asked if I thought I could render an objective opinion considering all the facts." He sipped at the Scotch he'd poured in preference to the coffee. "I told them the truth which was no, that I could not render an objective opinion about the mines. They asked me then if I thought Charlene, having been in on the investigation, could be impartial. I said yes; she has the job."

"You told them that after what she'd done?"

"I could have told them no, that she wasn't competent either, but that wouldn't have done you any good. They'd only have sent someone else in who wouldn't, I assure you, have gone to as much trouble as I. And, it would have been a lie. For all that Charlene is a personal thorn in my side, she is fair from a business point of view, and she was right in her estimation of my involvement. I had come in to town last night specifically to call the office first thing this morning." He polished off the Scotch in one gulp and swiveled his bar stool around to face her for the first time. "Shall I tell you what I was going to tell them, and why?"

She nodded. Nothing else would surprise her now.

"I was going to recommend that they close all the mines, every one of them, investigated or not, evidence or not, and do you know why? Last night I came to the conclusion that I would never have a chance with you as long as the mines lie between us. I'm not sure if I stand much of a chance anyway, I'm not sure if you're capable of letting go, but I thought if I could just close the mines, I might be able to get your mind off of them long enough to convince you that I was alive and *here* and willing to be a part of your life if only you'd let me.

Closing the mines seemed to be a small price to pay. It never once occurred to me that *I* wouldn't have to pay the price until they called and asked if I was objective about it." He shook his head. "I stepped down gracefully and it won't be held against me in future. As far as you're concerned, the mines will probably be closed. Charlene, as I've said, is fair and the evidence is there for everyone to see."

"I suppose she's fair for a back stabber," Honey muttered, glad she hadn't run into the "fair Charlene" so far, not sure if her control would extend itself that far. "So what now?"

"I'm a lame duck of sorts for three days until Charlene and I go back to Reno. I imagine I'll be reassigned then."

"Three days?" A not yet entirely formed idea nibbled at her brain. "I'd have three days to add to our cache of mine data, add to the number of mines your *fair* Charlene would be willing to consider?"

He followed her train of thought very well. "Not really. She'll have to leave Pahrump by tomorrow evening and she's not likely to stick around to the last second anyway. Besides, Teresa and Gerry will be needed here to help guide the equipment operators for the next few days, keep them from falling into the mines they're supposed to fill in along with the roads. And you can't go gallavanting around the desert on your own."

"I know." She caught at the one ray of hope he offered and held on to it tenaciously. "But I can't give up now."

He followed her out to the Bronco and watched her glance at the back to see its contents and climb in. "You can't go out there by yourself."

"I've been by myself for the last eighteen months, Turner. A few more days aren't going to matter one way or another. I have a promise I intend to keep to Daryl, and if I can't keep it, it won't be because I didn't try."

The door opened and slammed shut as Turner planted himself alongside her. "I can't vouch for my actions if you were tied up and couldn't move," he said. "But I think I'll go along and watch you like a hawk so you won't be alone." He leaned out the window and handed Indian a hastily scribbled note. "Do me a big favor, Indian, if you can."

Indian read the note quickly. "I can," he replied, not bothering to ask what the favor might be.

"If you don't hear from me by tomorrow evening, you get Charlene on a plane back to Reno with all the mine information we've got and this note, and make sure you tell her I'll make sure she never works again if she crosses me on this one. She owes me."

Gerry joined them at the window. "Are you both sure you know what you're doing? Do you have enough in the way of supplies?"

"Yes, and if not, we have the radio."

Even as he said it, Honey knew he hadn't looked, hadn't cared. He needed to come with her and anything else he might need would have to come later.

"We'll be back when we're done with the mines. I'll radio what information we gather as we go along until we're out of range. You can add that to Charlene's package, if we don't happen to be back by then."

"Happy hunting." Indian stepped back to let them pass, then put his hand on the Bronco's hood to prevent them from leaving. "Wait a minute." He removed the battered and always worn black leather hat from his head, fingering the single feather held in place by a snakeskin band. He brushed it free of dust lovingly and gave it to Turner.

"A welcome home gift for you. It has always brought me luck, and I think you will have need of luck handling that one," he admonished Honey gently through the window. "She can be a handful sometimes." He stood aside for them to go. "I'll moniter the radio."

Honey gunned the engine and headed out of town, secretly watching as Turner settled the hat comfortably on his head. It looked like it belonged there; he looked like he belonged here.

She forced herself to drive faster, keeping her thoughts on the road ahead rather than on the fact that he would be leaving at the end of their journey and there was nothing she could . . . or would . . . do to prevent it.

The roads leaving and coming into Pahrump were the only ones paved and kept in tip-top shape. The others were sometimes paved, sometimes not, turning into animal trails the further out one went until all that remained was a dirt track, hopefully free of the largest weeds, pitted with canyons and crevices left there by rare rain run off.

"Am I on course?" The Bronco's right front wheel rolled into one of the deeper ruts, throwing her off balance in his direction. She held onto the steering wheel, fighting it for control.

"Surprisingly enough, yes." He leaned closer to show her the map, following the tiny small scale squiggles with his finger. "If you're headed for these mines, along these mountains, you're on course."

"I am."

"Okay. Which do you intend to investigate first?"

Their talk centered around the mines until their conversation flowed easily, until the surface of things was smooth with nothing to indicate there might be turbulent undercurrents.

She checked a notebook in her pocket. "The mine we're after lies next to these mountains, on the edge of the dry lake, though the ground apparently isn't as dry as the name implies. The prospector hit water, not ore."

"Maybe he was after water." Turner took note of the increasing aridity around them. "It looks to me like water might be more precious than gold around here."

"The mine is supposed to be smack dab against the side of the mountain." She squinted to see something man-made in the distance. "And we should be fairly close."

"What about over there? Is that it do you think?" He pointed to what appeared to be a pile of wood that blended in with the mountainside not too far from where they were parked.

"Good eyesight." She complimented him as they drew alongside.

"I can see why nothing lives here." He wiped his face

with the corner of a red bandana and got out, surveying the remains of a wooden shack, its paint long since faded to a burnt pale yellow. They left the Bronco reluctantly, the area quiet as death without so much as a bird's song, only the wind that blew against the shaky boards of the shack, threatening to topple with every gust.

"It's unreal, a piece of the planet man has no business in."

"We have business here," she reminded him. "Though I can't say that I enjoy it either. And you thought the land you own was barren. Yours is an oasis compared to this."

He picked up the rotting door to the building, held in place by a thread of rusted hinge, and set it aside, ducking his head to avoid a portion of the roof, caved in at one point.

"Do you think that's wise?" she asked as he entered the one-room building, speaking to him from the safety of outside.

"I can't think of any other way to get a look at the mine, can you?"

"You could take my word for it, couldn't you? All you have to do to satisfy your ethics and your superiors is get a look at it, take a picture with a telephoto lens or something. Anyone can see this is dangerous. Are you from Missouri or something, Turner?"

"What?"

"The 'Show Me State,' you know, one of those people who have to see something before they believe it." She peeked inside to see him prodding at a portion of the dirt floor with a ceiling beam.

"I want to know exactly where the entrance is located."

Her heart fell to the very pit of her stomach as, without warning, the beam disappeared into a gaping hole that opened up in the floor. Turner let it fall and stepped back as it splashed into the water far below."

"Are you convinced yet?" she cried.

"Yep." He nodded with conviction. "You were right."

He brushed his hands on the back of his pants and left the shed. "There's water down there all right."

She threw him a mocking look. "It's a wonder you didn't feel duty bound to jump in and sample it."

"I told you I don't undertake the impossible, only the difficult. And I only attempt the difficult if there's a reasonable chance of my success, and a reward of some kind at the end." He tilted his head back toward the shed. *"That* is an impossibility, with no hope of a reward at the end unless you happen to need water, and we don't need water."

"Thankfully." She started to take the wheel again.

"Let me drive for a while," he offered. "The terrain is bad enough, but the sun reflecting up into your eyes is a killer."

"I don't mind the sun."

"I don't either; not if the sun is responsible for the color of your skin and the gold streaks in your hair." He tucked an errant strand behind one ear, fingering the lobe softly before removing his hand. "The sun is responsible for some very lovely things." He moved closer to where she stood. "Like the freckles on your nose and on your neck and on your back and your legs. You must sunbathe in the nude to get them in all those places."

"I do not," she contested. "And you're making all of it up. It was much too dark for you to tell…" She blushed, having broken her resolve not to mention that night to him again. "Turner, what are you doing?" It was no good pretending he was not trying to seduce her. *"Why* are you doing this?"

"I should think that would be obvious." He tilted his head to brush her forehead with his lips.

"Your subtle way of telling me work is done for the day before we've even begun?"

"I'm not a subtle man, Honeysuckle. I'm here because you wanted me here, because you wanted me to come. You know it and so do I. You knew before we left town that being out here, investigating the remaining mines, we'd be alone."

He unfastened the buttons on her shirt with swift and remarkable ease considering his eyes hadn't left her face.

"I hadn't counted on rape, Turner, and I haven't said yes to you yet."

"Only because I took the time to ask you if it was me you wanted. If I hadn't asked, you would be mine now in fact. You wouldn't be doubting me or the fact that you've fallen out of love with your husband and in love with me."

"No!" She would not stay to hear it spelled out.

"Yes." He prevented her from running again, capturing her face in between gentle and searching hands.

"I think that's what frightened you. You didn't want to face the fact that it was already too late, but you're going to face it now. Whether you leave your sterile solitary bed for mine or not doesn't count for anything now. You gave yourself to me willingly, and the only thing I didn't take from you was the opportunity to prove it. You gave me that opportunity by taking me along on this investigation."

Oh the vanity of the man! Damn him that he was right, at least in part, damn him that she wanted to have him love her as much as he wanted to do it. Damn him for making her think of him so often when it was becoming increasingly difficult to remember what Daryl had even looked like. It wasn't fair to take away the only thing Daryl had left of her, her thoughts, her body.

"I've given you nothing, unless you count lust as something more than transient. I don't love you," she denied, this lie hurting her less than the truth. "I'll admit that I want you. I'm human. But I won't forsake Daryl for that. When you leave, you won't take that last thing that I gave to him along with you." She rebuttoned her blouse, ashamed of the impulses that had allowed him free access there.

"So you want me to keep my distance from now on?" A muscle worked violently in his jaw. "You're telling me that I'm to think of having you as an impossibility? That I'm to take your word on it as final?"

"Yes." To say anything else would be to deny Daryl and all that he had once been to her. To bring this man as fully into her life as he would like to be would mean replacing Daryl altogether. Why must there be a choice? Couldn't she find a way to love them both? His expression told her otherwise.

"Yes, that's the way it has to be."

"Very well." He was quiet for a long time. "Remember it was what you wanted. You won't have to bother with my undesirable advances any more. There will be none."

She backed away from him and got into the passenger seat of the Bronco, staying as far on her own side as the car would allow, not even looking at him as he got in, as if his very gaze would burn her, though that was an illusion. He was a strong-willed man, and she was one of his impossibilities. From now on, no fire would burn in him for her. She had seen to that most effectively. He had finally taken her word for something. She hoped it was something she could learn to live with. She hoped he was someone she could learn to live without.

CHAPTER TEN

THEY WORKED STEADILY, silently through the day, minus the tea breaks and conversation that both made the work easier and slowed it down as well, stopping only long enough to allow one of them to call in to Indian with more information. Locations, detailed measurements, timber conditions, type of ore found... it all went out over the airways and hopefully to Charlene's growing list on the other end. Feeling as he did, Honey wondered why Turner bothered to try to close these obscure mines that had meaning only for her and perhaps for some future hiker who chanced to fall into one of them? A promise unfulfilled? If he was driven on by the same needs as she, he did not speak of it, but then he didn't speak at all, hadn't spoken more than a cursory word to her since this morning, and it was beginning to get on her nerves.

She whistled the tune to a popular song for her own amusement, reflecting that she had never heard the desert quite so quiet before, as if the tiny desert rodents, reptiles, and birds hesitated to scurry about and talk among themselves with their usual carefree clamor for fear of annoying the potential predator further or alerting him to their existence. She had to remind herself not to do the same thing, for he made her uneasy as well, remaining ominously silent and brooding through yet another uncomfortable meal, glaring up in irritation every time she reminded him in some small way that she was still there.

The sun set beautifully, displaying itself in a wash of color across the sky as it always did, ignored by them both this night. For two people determined not to pay much attention to one another, Honey didn't think either of them were paying much attention to anything else. For all that he would deny it, she could feel his eyes on her every time she turned her back, could feel his thoughts probing hers even when he was not looking. It had to stop. She couldn't endure another day of this. She slammed their pots and pans around as loudly as possible, resolutely deciding to stop the tiptoeing around on eggshells just because Turner was in a foul humor. What right had he to pass judgment on her decisions, on her chosen lifestyle? What right had he to make her miserable?

She washed their dishes in the clean sand, trying not to be contrite about her moral stand, her emotional stand, which had been in truth, almost as difficult for her to adopt as it had been for him to accept. The rubbing stopped, and she stared down at the pan in disgust, before throwing it in a childish display of temper across the fire, watching it land, with some satisfaction, squarely at his feet. The sunset wasn't the only thing that had gone unnoticed. Dinner too had fallen victim to their mutual inattention, with the result that at least half of it had scorched itself with apparent permanency to the bottom of the pan.

"I'm getting some water to wash with unless you want to eat the remains of tonight's meal tomorrow, too." She dared him to deny her.

"Heaven forbid. I'm in enough danger of food poisoning the way it is."

He was lucky she didn't have another pan handy to throw at him.

"Smart man," she mumbled testily on her way to the back of the Bronco. "I should let *him* do all the cooking. Inept city rat, so used to eating in restaurants he'd probably burn water..."

She lifted the back window of the vehicle and threw the tarp back from their small hoard of supplies. Indian and Gerry had obviously packed with the same haste she and Teresa had that last day. Everything lay in a jumble. She moved the boxes and bags aside searching for their extra water, housed in blue plastic five-gallon containers. She lifted the jugs that were there, leaving the full, not-to-be-touched five gallon reserve and extracting the one they had opened yesterday. She swished the contents around judging how much it held, hoping it held enough to wash the pans. They would be home tomorrow if Turner kept his house-afire pace, and all but the most hard to reach mines were done anyway. There would be enough water, if she counted their reserve to get them home easily.

She poured the entire amount of the one jug into a plastic tub, and going for their pots and pans, swept away with them to a private spot on the other side of the Bronco where she wouldn't have to endure any of Turner's silent or verbal antagonism.

The easier pots out of the way, and the stubborn pan set to soak, she was about to throw the water away when it occurred to her that perhaps there was still another service the water could perform... a double and perhaps a triple duty.

She scratched her head, watching the sand drift down on her shoulders like so much untidy dandruff. Out of necessity and a shortage of drinking water while away from home, she, along with the rest of them, hadn't bathed beyond a simple wash up, or washed her hair or her clothes in days. It was one of the drawbacks of camping out in a land where water had to be used for drinking and precious little else. But now that the water was here and no longer drinkable, she had other plans for it besides throwing it away.

Her eyes darted to Turner on the other side of the Bronco, his back to the fire which was also between them. Unless tonight proved an exception to today, he wouldn't stir himself to bother her. It was a snap decision and it took only a few moments to shuck her clothing and step into the small tub of cold soapy water. The conditions were less than optimum, but a sunken tub filled to the brim with hot bath oil permeated, perfumed water at any other time could not have seemed as luxurious as this bath did to her now. If she was careful, she could wash herself and her hair and have enough water left to do a passable job on her clothes, some of them anyway, and if she felt like it, some of Turner's too. She tossed her shirt, bra, and panties into the water at her feet to presoak while she combed the water through her hair, small moans of pleasure emanating from her throat as it trickled down her scalp and onto her face, making tiny rivulets in the layers of dust and sand that had accumulated there during the day. Using the dish rag, she scrubbed the whole of her until her skin fairly glowed a healthy and very clean pink.

The night had turned cold, and she was ready at last to end her pleasurable but cold bath in favor of the crackling fire Turner had started, when a noise from the Bronco caught her attention.

"Are you the proprietress of this laundry?"

She had no idea how long he had been standing there, but he looked fairly well ensconced in his position at the back of the Bronco. His glance flickered over her shoulders to the dripping clothing she had hung on a low bush, but it soon came back to her, standing only a bit over ankle deep in the tub of much used water. Her skin was covered with gooseflesh from the cold, its surface damp and glistening with water, and she could only hope he would attribute its pink blush to her persistent scrubbing.

"If you'll leave your laundry over there..." She pointed to a spot several yards away. "...I'll do it for you." Actually she hadn't yet decided whether she was in a forgiving enough mood to do his laundry, but it would be worth the extra effort if he would just go back to the fire and not watch her with those hungry dark eyes, so full of yearning and denial that it was hard to look away. She wet her lips and swallowed, her eyes growing wide as he slowly made his way over to her bath.

"Haven't you heard of women's rights?" He spoke to her in an entirely normal tone of voice, something she doubted her own ability to do. "It's no problem for me to wash my own clothes. I'm used to it, though I must admit I generally do them in a washer and me in the shower. Still, one must make do." He stripped his shirt off, pulling it over his head slowly to reveal a muscular chest that looked even better in the flesh than it did in her memory. He walked with an easy animal grace closer to her, his stride liquid and unconsciously sexual. The pants came next, sliding off his hips and to the ground with pockets and cuffs full of sand. His clothes were every bit as scroungy as hers were; it was only natural that he would want to wash them; he wasn't doing this male striptease to tease her; she'd told him she wasn't interested; *why was he doing this to her?* She ran through the list of arguments mentally in a flash.

The breath caught in her throat as his hands fastened themselves to her hips, his fingers unmoving, yet still having an effect.

"Well? Do you come out or do I have to try to fit in there with you?"

"I'm coming out," she replied anxiously, wishing she'd had the foresight to get a towel from the Bronco before taking her bath. The hands she used to cover her breasts were far from large enough to do the job adequately, and they left other areas of her person immodestly bare, making her wish she hadn't tried to cover herself in the first place.

"The first step..." He coached her in a soft coercing voice, "is to move your feet, like this." He stepped into the now much too small tub beside her, his thighs brushing hers. "Unless you're good at levitation or . . . unless you've changed your mind about me and decided to stay?"

"No." She maneuvered past him, her retreat any other way blocked by the creosote bush she'd used as a clothesline. "I'm going." Her hands, still between them at her breasts, brushed against the dark hair that covered his chest, so sensuous in its masculinity, so different from her. If things had been otherwise, she would have liked to hold him close and feel that sprinkling of chest hair tickle her skin, she would have laid her head against him and smelled the heady aroma of his skin mixed with the soap and the sage that permeated his clothes. It was an arousing thought that she dared not dwell on long.

She hopped out of the tub with as much cool dignity as she could muster, which wasn't an awful lot, and went for a change of clothes. She unfolded two towels and set one of them on the Bronco's shorter antenna, looking up only to see him covered in foamy lather. She closed her eyes and left to dress by the fire. Morality and guilt and love all mixed together were not an easy combination to live with.

"How about some coffee?" The towel wrapped about his hips with a questionable security, he knelt on the sleeping bag to warm himself beside the fire. "You live in a land of extremes. How the temperature can drop this low when it gets hot enough to melt the rubber on my tennis shoes during the day, I don't know."

"Things are like that out here. You get used to it." She was glad for the conversation. It meant he'd decided against the meaningful silences. It meant that the cold war they were having was, if not entirely over, at least blessedly postponed.

"I don't agree. Most things can't get used to it. They die out. The ones that survive live on the very edge of existence. Like you."

"Pardon?" She handed him a cup of instant coffee.

"I've been thinking that you're very like this desert yourself and its inhabitants."

"Barren and lifeless?" She tried to make a joke of it
and could not.

"Perhaps . . . for a time."

Here was no gentleman. She would have preferred
him to lie, but it was not his way.

"But during the spring, after the bitterness of the winter has gone, and before the summer comes along to dry
her sources of life up, I imagine this desert bursts forth
with so much beauty and so much life. I'm sure it's
worth enduring all the rest just to see it. The plants that
just barely make it when the desert can offer them nothing
to sustain life must go crazy when spring comes."

"It is beautiful," she agreed, hoping it was her over
active imagination that was reading more into his comments than was on the surface. "And the contrast is so
sharp, it makes the beauty all the more vivid."

"The parallels are astounding. No wonder you like it
here so much."

"Don't you like it here?" she asked curiously. He was
planning to go away, but he seemed to fit in so well.

"I don't think I'm hardy enough to live on the very
edge of existence, waiting for a moody desert to succor
my needs. I don't know if I could live with fire one
moment and ice the next."

How could she answer that, now that she was sure
he wasn't talking about the desert verbena and cactus.
She didn't answer him, staring into the fire instead, feeling the heat on the outside and the ice on the inside just
as the desert that he could not live with did.

"Good night, Honey." He pulled the sleeping bag up
and around his shoulders, settling himself in for the night.

The desert had reversed itself by morning, the iciness
of the night before melting in the scorching 98-degree
heat that was present by eight A.M.

"I'm glad this is our last day." She helped Turner to
pack as speedily as possible.

"We'll hope this is our last day. I'm making no promises." He soaked a large blue handkerchief in water and

folding it into a long band, tied it around his head, setting his own leather hat on top, and leaving Indian's on the seat. "The terrain from here on in is bad, and though I'm sure we'd make better time out of four-wheel drive, I don't want to risk getting stuck out here, not when we're out of radio contact."

"We're out of radio contact?" She had known they would be, but it was an eerie feeling nonetheless to be out of contact with the outside world.

"Yes. I tried to call Indian this morning and all I raised was some static. They could be reading us, without us being able to reach them, but I don't think so."

"We'll be extra careful then." She packed the remaining pieces of their equipment into the Bronco.

"Chin up." He dropped Indian's lucky hat onto her head. "Wear this for luck and by tonight we should be back home."

"Sounds good to me." That wasn't quite true. Home meant, among other things, that he would be leaving.

The day wore on, the mines difficult to reach and more difficult to explore, especially now that extra care must be taken. They tried the radio off and on but there was nothing but static for them to hear. They climbed back into the Bronco after lunch and made their way over ground more rugged and rocky than any they had encountered so far.

"Where's our next stop?"

"Just over the next rise. You know that. Why?" His eyes were on the ground ahead of them and not where hers were... on the temperature gauges.

"We're running hot." It was not a thing to be terribly worried about. The terrain had been very rough and the Bronco was after all a machine, not a mountain goat.

They climbed the rise carefully and coasted down, running on a smoother surface for a time, but by the time they reached the next mine and rolled to a stop, threads of steam were curling up from beneath the hood along with a faint hissing sound.

Turner sucked in a pained breath and let loose with

a string of oaths as his hand found the broken radiator hose and its escaping steam.

"Can it be repaired?" Honey looked over his shoulder, wanting to see for herself.

"It isn't too bad. Do you have any tape?"

She dug into the glove compartment and fished out the tape he'd asked for. "Will this do?"

"Yes."

But it didn't, and it didn't take very long for them to discover that it didn't. This time steam belched out volcanolike when he lifted the hood.

"Can it be fixed?" she asked him again, forgetting the cardinal rule women have known since cars were invented, that being: never talk to a man who's "fixing" one.

"Sure." He growled sarcastically. "Get the damned thing to your nearest garage and it'll be fixed up in no time. But unless you want to go for the tow truck on foot, you'd best move out of my way and let me see what I can do."

"Oh, for Pete's sake." She shouldered her way in next to him, all rules aside. "Let me see. I know the Bronco better than you do. I think all we need is enough black tape. You can't fix a leak like this with a Band-Aid, you know." She unrolled more of the tape, separating the long length from its roll with her teeth, and wrapped it securely in place around the hose.

"You think that's going to hold?" He added water from their reserve to the radiator and capped it off.

"I think so." She added a silent second to that. If it didn't, she'd never live it down.

They continued on, slower than before, their eyes on the gauges in front of them, especially the temperature gauge which crept with a sickening certainty to the hot side.

"Of all the miserable, lousy, rotten things to go wrong..."

"We're in trouble." She admitted defeat as they inspected the now nearly split in two radiator hose, covered with a stinking, sticky black layer of melted tape and rubber. "And I don't think we have anything to repair this kind of break." She went through the back of the Bronco looking for anything that might be used to repair the hose, to no avail; down filled sleeping bags, tinned and dried food, tools, boxes of samples and written material, books, all specialized for a certain need, none of which could fill the need they were faced with now.

"We don't have anything."

"Maybe not . . ." He hesitated. "But maybe we do." He plucked his own leather hat from on top of his head. "You said a Band-Aid wouldn't do, but what about a leather-and-tape Band-Aid?"

"Your hat?"

He shrugged. "I never liked it much. I prefer Indian's. Besides it's going for a worthy cause." He dissected it with the bowie knife at his belt and fashioned a covering for the leaky hose.

"We're not home yet." She didn't share his satisfied look when the job was done. "We'll still have to nurse this turkey along, and I have a feeling if we stick to our original plan, we won't get very far."

"Sour grapes. It'll hold," he decided confidently.

"Well, just in case it doesn't." She unfolded a map from the front seat and lay it over the hood. "Whether we go backwards or forwards along our planned route, we'll have to climb along the way somewhere. The engine will have to work harder and we'll use a lot of water, if the hose holds. Whereas if we go this way . . ." She drew a line away from their original penciled in course. ". . . we should be on even ground within a couple of miles, and it's all downhill from there back to town. We should be able to use less water."

"But no one will know where we are if we don't make it back to town or within radio range of town."

"In a nutshell, yes." She slumped against the hood, unsure, trying to decide what their best alternative might be. "Here's how it is." She shared their options with him as she saw them. "We can either use more of our reserve water for the radiator and try to make it back, or we can pack it in right here and wait until someone comes out to find us."

"I'm more independent than that, and a great deal more self-reliant." He scratched the last option from her list as she'd hoped he would. "But I wouldn't like to stake my life on the hope that the hose is going to hold if we continue to push the engine like we've been doing. If the roads were even...Lord, if there were roads at all, it would be better, but we're asking her to be part bulldozer and with a busted hose at that. I say we get off the rocks and down onto the flat lands. We'll use up to half of the reserve water we have left and then drive her till she drops."

"Off the original course?" She wanted to be very sure she was reading him correctly.

"I think it's the only hope we have of making it back on our own, and frankly, I don't know if we'd have enough water to wait it out until someone gets suspicious and comes looking for us."

"We're due back tonight. We've got plenty of water to last until then. You only need a gallon a day per person if you're not doing anything too strenuous, and I figure, if we don't get back by tonight, they'll give us another twenty-four hours, but then they'll come looking."

He groaned in guilt, hindsight taunting him. "They'd come out for us within twenty-four hours after tonight, *if* our deadline to be back was tonight, but it isn't. I told Indian and Charlene, in the note, not to worry if we didn't show up for several days. I hoped to be back in time to hand her our notes in person and put her on the plane, or failing that, call in time to give her the facts before the presentation. But I asked her if she would include these dozen or so mines in her presentation anyway, include them in her recommendation if it was her decision to close them."

"*You* asked her to lie?" The implications of that fact hit her harder than the fact that they could be out here much longer than she had anticipated.

"Not exactly. I gave her the coordinates of these mines and all the facts we knew before coming out here. I suppose I did ask her to bend the truth if she had to, if I hadn't gotten in touch with her. But I expected to be in touch with her before then. I still expect to." He was uncomfortable with the admission.

She looked at him with new eyes. How much was he willing to sacrifice to close these mines for her, for she didn't think he was trying to close them for any other reason.

"So you're telling me we could be out here for several more days before anyone gets too worried and comes looking? I think if I had to do it all over again, I'd opt for dirty dishes, dirty hair, no bath, and a few extra gallons of water," she said, bemoaning yesterday's luxury out loud.

"Let's not be too dramatic, all right? We do have our two half-full canteens, right?" He marked them down on a notepad along with their other information. "And I saw a bottle of beer in the back... probably Indian's."

"No doubt." She agreed dryly, remembering the old man's penchant for warm brew. "It's not the best idea, drinking a diuretic in this heat, but I guess if Indian's been doing it for years, we can do it for one bottle... if you drink it."

"Thanks a lot." He continued with the list. "We also have a few cans of orange soda... warm also, and what we have left of the reserve. That should hold us."

"If we don't use up any more water in the radiator and if the hose doesn't break completely. If those things don't happen, we won't need the liquid we do have. And if they do..."

"They wouldn't dare." He pounded his fist on the four-wheel drive in warning. "This beast has already eaten my second-best hat. It wouldn't dare break down after that."

But it did, sometime after they had crossed the rugged terrain and found their way to even ground, and this time there was no humor or any attempt at it by either of them. This was serious.

"The leather didn't hold?" She allowed him to inspect the damage for the third time before asking.

"It's not the leather. It's the rest of the hose disintegrating under the heat and pressure further along the first split." He pushed the headband up to keep the sweat out of his eyes. "And I don't know how long the tape I mickey moused together will hold either, certainly not anywhere near long enough to get us back to town."

"Then we wait for them to find us. They *will* find us." She had worked with Search & Rescue long enough to know, too long to lose her faith in the people and their capabilities now.

"The trouble is going to be in waiting for them . . . and waiting for them to find us, unless you know of some way to boost the radio signal or you know of a water hole we can reach on foot from here."

She thought for a moment. "I'm not sure about the radio signal; I don't think so though, that was Teresa's specialty. But as for the water hole, I think I can solve our water problem and put us in a good location to be found, too."

"Don't keep me in suspense, Honey. You have my full attention."

The idea that had wormed its way into her thoughts was not appealing, but it might be more appealing than their alternatives. She dug the map out again. "We're close to the mud flats . . . the dry lake, as the crow flies. If we cross here . . ." She drew an imaginary line, bisecting their original circular route. "We could reach, or come close to reaching, the mine with the water in the bottom, remember?"

"I wish that wasn't one of the options."

"But we'd be back on track then as well as near water. We could be located faster."

"I'll have to revise my concept of impossibility, but I have to admit, I wouldn't mind being wrong in this case. If you think we can get the water out, it's worth a try."

His seal of approval was all that she had been waiting for to solidify her own position. She tried not to think about why what he had to say was so important to her. It suggested an intimacy they could not have, an intimacy that would come to an end at any rate when they were found and he went back to the world he lived in and she stayed here, dutifully bound to a place and a way of life that she had committed herself to long before Turner came along to disrupt it.

"This much and no more." He poured the allotted two gallons carefully into the radiator, scrupulously avoiding the spillage of a single precious drop. "When this runs out..." He stressed the when and not the if of it. "...that's where it stays. We can't afford after that to feed its thirst and not our own."

It was agreed, and they drove, if not as easily as the crow flies, at least they traveled in that direction, the soft continual hissing from beneath the hood a constant reminder that if they did not reach a sanctuary soon, only the warm beer, orange soda, and a few gallons of water would stand between them and the lethal, dehydrating effects of the desert summer heat.

That thought made her thirsty, and knowing that their water was in a drastically limited supply made her thirstier still.

"Think of something else," Turner warned her, reading her mind most accurately.

"What?" She was in no state of mind to be creative.

"Something pleasant. Anything to divert your mind."

She leaned back in the seat, letting her hair fall behind, and closed her eyes in concentration. "Something pleasant. Let me think. How about this—an Olympic-sized pool with a fountain in the middle that splashes water all over the rest. And a pool chair inside complete with a styrofoam table full of icy margaritas?"

"Sounds great, but I don't think you've diverted yourself from being thirsty. Kind of like trying to diet and not think of fattening food while working in a candy store."

She wondered what he thought about to divert his mind from the slish-sloshing of the water container in back, for surely he was as thirsty as she, his lips dry and slightly chapped already. Yet it didn't seem to be bothering him. "How do you manage it?" She looked under his seat. "Do you have a secret cache of popsicles that you're holding out on me?"

"No. I have my private fantasies to occupy my thoughts." He did not invite inquiring questions. "And I have a positive outlook. We're having a bit of bad luck, you and I, but I'm not ready to toss in the towel yet. I won't declare us a lost cause until every last bit, every shred of hope I have has been used up."

She was never sure if anything he said held one meaning or more, but she was glad to have his optimism, especially when the steam began to billow from the radiator with a screaming whistle as it escaped. Even then, he drove tenaciously until the temperature indicator had flattened itself against the end of the temperature gauge's hot side.

"End of the line, Honeysuckle. Everyone out." He shut the grateful engine off before it seized and refused to turn itself over ever again, indicating he had high hopes of getting it running at some later date.

"Shall we get started?" He saw no reason to put off the inevitable.

The desert floor loomed up ahead, overwhelming in its vastness. "I don't suppose we could wait?"

"For what?" he asked. "There are a few things we need to do here first, but time is of the essence, wouldn't you say?"

Yes, she would say, but it was awesome to contemplate venturing out into all that stretched before them on foot, leaving nearly everything they possessed behind. She appraised their breakdown site when they finished making preparations, and she was glad of the Bronco's bright paint. Without it, all sign of them could easily be covered, erased by a single and not too severe sand storm.

He shrugged on a backpack and surveyed their work along with her. "Can you think of anything we might have missed?"

"I don't think so. You left a note on the front seat telling what happened and what our plans are now?"

"Yes."

"And we've got everything we need with us? The water? Ropes? Food? Sleeping bags? Radio? First aid kit?" She ran down the emergency list and to each he nodded, rechecking its location in either his backpack or hers. Everything necessary was there, but their resources as they agreed they had "everything" seemed pitifully few.

"Stand back." He pulled a match from his pack and lit one of their gasoline drenched tires as a signal, sending up columns of billowing dark smoke for searchers to zero in on and follow. The only problem was, when the searchers traced the smoke down, they would be long gone.

CHAPTER ELEVEN

HONEY HAD REVISED her opinion of what was necessary by early on the next morning, eliminating some of the equipment they had deemed essential the day before. The seemingly inadequate amount of supplies in the packs had grown, if not in size, then surely in weight, or so it seemed to her aching and raw shoulder blades. The pack that had felt so comfortable at home for an afternoon's excursion into the mountains, now grated against the material of her blouse and dug painfully into her flesh.

Turner saw the shady clump of cactus before she did, but only seconds before, and she reached it first, their thoughts, their actions finely tuned to their mutual needs, without the need for words.

"What time is it?" she asked as they dropped their packs to the sand and proceeded to rest against them. Time had ceased to have much meaning for her some hours ago, the passage of minutes and hours no longer the deciding factor in when they might expect to eat or rest or . . . drink.

"Two." Even speaking unnecessarily had become an effort, their tongues clumsy in mouths too dry too long. And what was there to say except that it was hot and she was tired and thirsty and sore and disheartened? He must feel these things too and wouldn't need reminding.

He pulled out their dwindling supply of liquid that had sounded adequate yesterday. The formula was a gallon to two gallons of water per day for each person doing moderate amounts of exercise. They hadn't allowed themselves the luxury of drinking that much, they could not have allowed themselves that much, making do with a cup full now and then, but it had been a hard sacrifice. Honey had the impression that even if they had consumed all the water the survival booklets said they would need, they would still have been thirsty.

"How much do we have left?"

"One gallon of water, two cans of orange soda . . . and bad news, we broke the bottle of beer somehow along the way."

"You didn't want to drink the beer anyway," she consoled him.

"I've changed my mind."

"So have I." She didn't remind him that he had been carrying the beer when it broke. She'd fallen enough times herself, tripping over rocks that seemed to jump up to catch her feet, tossing her and all that she carried onto the ground. In a little over twenty-four hours they had used up half of their meagre supply of water, gotten only a quarter of the amount they should have had, and who knew how long it might be until they reached the mine or someone reached them?

"Tell you what . . ." She proposed the plan. "My legs are ready to drop off at any second. Why don't we go through the packs one more time and see if we can't get rid of some of this excess weight. We could even lighten the load a little bit by sharing a can of soda while we do it. What do you say?"

"I say . . . I'm too thirsty to argue." There was a note of desperation in his agreement that bothered her.

Despite their best intentions, they drained the can in less than a minute, Turner licking the last bubbly drops from his lips with regret.

"I will never, ever again complain about or take tap water for granted. I'd drink pool water now, chlorine and sediment, suntan oil and all."

"I thought we weren't going to talk about water." She stretched out on the sand and, closing her eyes for a brief moment of rest, lay her head on one of the packs. "Think about whatever it is you meditate on when you don't want to think about water, and while you're at it, let me in on your secrets. I'm fresh out of ideas."

"You wouldn't appreciate it." He changed the subject abruptly. "How much further do you think we have to walk?"

"It's a big park." She shrugged. "We were at the end of it before this happened, and we set out cross country. I don't know how many miles an hour we average . . . not much . . . but I'd guesstimate we have another day and a half, maybe two before we reach the shack and the water."

"Think how nice it would be if Indian was there when we arrived."

"He's not going to wait there if we aren't there," she reasoned. "He'll check it and go on until he finds our Bronco and the note; then he'll track us to the mine, which will take longer."

"I'd like to get there before he does then and wait."

She lifted her head from the pack. "We could go faster without the packs."

He dismissed that idea with a wave of his hand. "We need the packs."

She fingered the sturdy frame. The sleeping bag she carried and the empty pack together probably weighed twenty pounds. How much faster could they go minus twenty pounds? Fast enough to get them to the mine before Indian perused it and went on, hoping to find them elsewhere?

"We don't need two packs," she argued. "Only the

contents of the two packs, and not all of those. We can whittle more of the contents away, I'm sure, and we don't need two sleeping bags. I mean, it would be crowded, but we'd be warm and there would be less to carry. Best of all, we could alternate carrying it."

"I'm not a cold-blooded reptile, Honey," he rasped at her. "You were the one who insisted on a hands-off policy. Don't change it now unless you're ready to change how you feel, correction, how you *think* you feel along with it!"

Her cheeks flamed at the innuendo that she might not know her own mind, that she might not be able to live up to her own convictions. She didn't want him to be right. "I *had* thought of it, of how it might appear if we slept . . . well . . . together in the same bag, but I assumed we were both rational human beings."

"I'm not sure how long I'm going to be rational, and I already feel more like an animal than a human being, so leave it be, will you?"

"For God's sake Turner, this isn't exactly by choice! We're out here, stranded without transportation, without enough water or food, and all you can think of is *sex?* I can't believe you're real. What are you thinking of?"

He was over her in a flash, pushing her forcefully against the nylon pack with a power she hadn't known he possessed, kissing her without any of the restraint he had shown before. She struggled to free herself. An animal indeed, and one she was alarmed to admit who aroused her greatly.

"I've been thinking of you," he answered her between kisses. "I've thought of precious little else since this started. It's what I've fantasized over when the desire for a drink of water becomes all consuming. The only other thing I've ever experienced which is as maddening is you! The only thing that can wipe out every other thought, every other need is the memory of your bare skin touching mine, your fingers arousing me, touching me, the thought of what it might have been like if you hadn't run away . . ." His breathing came in short, heavy puffs, his eyes half closed, undressing her with their frank stare. "And here you go suggesting we sleep platonically together. I doubt you could do it, but I'd get the blame if anything happened. And I'd have to be more than thirsty to keep my hands off you, woman; I'd have to be dead!"

She pushed against him, hoping to find a vulnerable moment. "And you just might end up that way if you don't knock it off. I'm in no mood to be nice. You're no gentleman to keep reminding me of that night. I thought I knew what I was doing, but I was wrong. It was wrong, at least it was wrong for me."

"You insist on thinking of me as a gentleman just because I came from the city and dressed like one. I'm no gentleman and it's time you learned that; I'm just a man, and you didn't act like it was wrong that night. You acted like a woman who hasn't been loved by a man in a long time and you wanted to be loved again . . . badly. What's wrong with that?"

"How dare you!"

"How dare I, you ask? I dare because I'm sick of you deluding yourself, and I dare because it's true. I know what a woman's body feels like when she's ready for my loving."

"You're disgusting!" she screamed at him, covering her ears with her hands to prevent any more of the damaging truth to seep in, but he removed them and held them in his hands.

When he spoke again, his voice had lost its violence. "I'm disgusting because I want you and you want me in return? That sounds like one of Pauline's sermons. It doesn't sound like it came from you."

A single tear of disillusionment trickled from one eye and slid down her face, as if she was reluctant to give up even that small bit of body moisture.

"I can't deny that . . . that you make me feel in a way I haven't felt in a long, long time. I had a good sex life and I miss it . . . my body misses it, but my heart misses more than just sex, my heart can't give up the love I had

with him just for the sake of physical satisfaction. And
that's all you are to me, a way to satisfy a physical need.
I could just as easily..."

"No. Don't say it." He covered her mouth with his
hand. "Don't say it because you don't mean it, and I
can't take any more right now. If you degrade what we
had, what we almost had one more time with that hogwash you've been spouting, I don't know what I'll do,
but it's likely to be violent."

He picked up the remaining articles from her pack
and dropping them inside the pockets of his own, shouldered it and strode steadily away from her without a
word.

And so they walked, side by side, for more hours than
she wanted to keep track of, his step less lively than
before, his energy low. Had she taken away something
more than his pride; had she stripped him of his hope,
his spirit as well?

That night Turner fell into a fitful sleep, his back to
the woman who he thought cared about him not at all.

"I love you Turner." She breathed the admission whis-
per-soft so that even if he was awake, only she could
hear the secret. She could admit it for what it was worth,
for all that it couldn't change her course of action, to
herself at last.

"Honey, wake up." The voice in her dreams was much
more inviting than its waking counterpart and it took a
few minutes before the real Turner overode the other.

"I want to get going before it gets any hotter. Please
get up."

This time the cold command was accompanied by a
rough hand and she had no other choice but to listen to
it.

"I'm getting, I'm getting." She crawled out of the bag
reluctantly and accepted the can of cling peaches he offered her, savoring its juice as the last she might enjoy
for some time.

"Did you eat?" She thought he might not have, saving
the peaches for her.

"Yes."

Just that. One word and still it said so much. A part of her, the disloyal part longed to put the spark back into his voice, the sparkle back into his eyes, but even if she might have considered it, there was no time. He set out this day with as much silent determination as he had yesterday, leaving her to follow him and keep up as best she might.

"Let me carry the pack for a while, huh?" She caught up with him, noticing how his posture had slumped and his feet slowed, which accounted for her catching up with him, after several hours.

"No."

"I'm not a child." Though she did feel like one, running after him trying to elicit some kind of intelligent response other than a simple, unreasonable "no."

"I know you're not a child; you're a woman . . . ." He added with a look to her body, ". . . however much you try to deny it. I, on the other hand, am a man and I'm not about to let you trudge along carrying a forty-pound pack while I walk alongside without one."

"That's stupid!" she declared. "What do you think I've been doing since this morning? I thought we agreed to share the burden?"

"We didn't *agree* to anything."

"Have we ever agreed on anything?" She was beginning to have her doubts.

"We almost did . . . once."

Would he never forget that night? On the other hand, she didn't think she would willingly let go . . . or strip him of . . . anything that could, by the mere thinking of it, drive the terrible thirst away.

The day wore on, and they shared what water was left to them. She felt wretched, but thought he felt worse. The pack, though lighter as the day wore on and their water vanished, was still a heavy thing on his back.

"Please let me take it," she offered again after one of their more frequent rest stops.

He did not bend to pick it up as she was sure he would. "For a little while, but not for long."

As much as she wanted to relieve him, she was glad he'd added the stipulation. She wasn't sure how long she could carry it.

"What's that?" Honey stopped after they had gone but a short distance, hoping her eyes weren't playing tricks, just to allow her a few moment's respite from the mountain she felt she carried on her back. "Is that a building? Is that *the* building?"

"I don't know. Maybe." Turner scanned the map, one of the few things they had not economized on and discarded. They had walked for a long time, always in the general direction of the mine/water hole, but rarely keeping themselves finely attuned to exactly how far ahead it might be for fear the discouragement of knowing would be too great.

He checked their position on the map against the compass reading and squinted at the building in the hazy distance. "I think it is."

They had walked forever, farther than forever, and suddenly the thought of the shady building and the water underneath was a goal worth reaching as soon as possible. She started to run, the pack no longer a deterring factor, nothing stopping her until she felt a hand at her back.

"Steady." Turner commanded. "Walk. If it's the building, and I think it is, it'll still be there when we get there. You can't run in this heat, not after all we've been through. You'll collapse and I can't carry you."

She could see the sense in that, but the waiting was terrible. "Do you think I could have a drink?" Surely there could be no harm in that now since the water they had walked too long to reach was almost within reach.

He gave her what was left of the flask he carried, and she considered draining it altogether, leaving them both with only the one half-empty canteen, but she stopped herself without quite knowing why and took only a few swallows, then wiped the mouth of the flask with her shirt and handed it to him.

"No." He refused it, and contrary to his own advice, broke into a run the last few hundred yards, entering the ruined mine area with something approaching glee.

"I didn't think we'd ever make it! No, I knew we'd make it, I just didn't know when." He drank from his own canteen then, deeply, as if he had promised himself not to do so until they had reached their goal. "Let's fill these, shall we?"

They approached the dilapidated shack with a great deal more enthusiasm this time than last, pushing the rock tailings aside to get a better view of the shaft.

"Be careful," she warned him. "The floor in here isn't all that solid, remember?"

"I will."

"How far down do you think the water is?"

"I couldn't tell," he admitted. "But we heard it, didn't we?" He unrolled a long length of rope from his pack and, tying a metal cup to its end, threw it over the edge of the opening, uncoiling it slowly and listening as it slid over the gravel, descending down the incline, deeper and deeper into the bowels of the shaft until, like a fish swimming out to sea with the hook in its mouth, the cup fell, taking the rope with it into the abyss below.

It was a long, long way down; they could hear the metal cup as it clanged against the rock walls of the shaft, and still it fell until there was no more rope to unwind.

"Did we hit it?" She listened intently for the sound of the cup splashing into water, but it was too far below ground to be sure, and the wind blowing through the walls of the shack made its own form of music to drown out the sound they strained to hear.

He didn't have an answer for her, bringing the rope up slowly, his face set, his muscles tense with the waiting. But when the cup finally appeared, it was dry.

Turner touched the cup hopefully, searching for water that wasn't there. "Get your rope. We'll tie the two together. There's water down there, I heard it, and it can't be too much farther down."

If she had had the tears to cry, she would have shed buckets of them, but there were no tears, only dry frightened sobs. "We left my rope somewhere along the way."

"So damned close and yet so far." He mouthed the cliché and threw the cup against the far wall, sending a tremor along its frame.

"What do we do now?" She had come to look to him for answers, and he had provided them, arrogantly assured of himself. He did not answer her now. Finally after a few minutes he sighed.

"We can try to raise Indian on the radio, and we can wait."

Even more endless and frustrating than walking with the goal miles and miles away, waiting without being able to take any positive action at all was worse. They took turns calling out over the airways until neither of them could stand the sight of the radio or the sound of the static, they played games of "hang-man" in the sand until neither of them could think of a new word for the other to guess at, and still they waited, noticing for once the slow panorama of the sun as it set in the western sky, noticing the soft skittering of the native animals, noticing each other most of all.

Deciding that the hut could collapse in on them at any moment, they erected a shelter of some wood that was already down, covering the rough lean-to with a "moon blanket" from the pack. It had been too light and compact to throw away.

They lay on the opened sleeping bag together, underneath the concave moon blanket canopy, quiet, listening to the quiet. They discussed everything from politics to pigs and all that lay in between to pass the time until there was nothing left to talk about save those taboo subjects neither of them had broached: she and he and Daryl and the crazy mixed-up feelings that forced her to love them both and prevented her from loving them both too.

"How long do you think it will be until they find us?" she asked idly, well able to figure it out for herself.

"A few days if we're unlucky."

"And how much water do we have?"

"A few cups I guess." He turned his head to look at her lying next to him. "What are you getting at?"

She sat up cross legged, her head brushing the top of the moon blanket. "Just this. The radio should be working here, because it worked here before, but it doesn't. I dropped it so many times it's hardly surprising, but now that it doesn't, we can't count on it to bring help. We're going to have to wait until help finds us, and for all we know, Indian could already have checked this place out and gone on, or he might not be looking for us at all yet. In either case, we're going to have to help ourselves. And I'm still thinking the water in the mine is our best bet. I was thinking we could tear up the sleeping bag and the moon blanket and tie them into the rope, just see if the added length would help us reach the water."

He stroked her dark gold hair, lanky now from not being washed, but still beautiful to him. "I know you're thirsty, but that isn't a good idea, Honey. The moon blanket is the only real shade we have, and you know as well as I do it isn't anywhere near strong enough to hold any weight. And it would be...ironic...if they found us and the heat hadn't gotten to us, but exposure to cold had because we tore up the sleeping bag."

"Do you really think that's likely to happen?"

"I just don't see tearing our sleeping bag or the shelter up when we need them both and we don't know if doing so would reach the water."

"Turner, I can't sit here idle anymore. I'll go nuts. What else do we have that could be used to add onto the rope?"

"Straps from the pack." He didn't join in her "do-something-even-if-it's-wrong" spirit. "Other than that, all we have are the clothes on our backs, a little food, the first aid kit. It's not much to work with."

"Our clothes." She grabbed at the idea. "We could use our clothes and the pack straps." If it would help bring the water up, her clothes could go and gladly. She would have taken a chapter from a fairy tale and mimicked Rapunzel if her hair would have done any good.

This time he made no comment on the intimacy her idea might bring about. "I don't think it's going to do us any good."

"But you don't *know* that," she insisted. "The water can't be much farther down." If it was, she was not ready to admit that it was without another attempt. "We don't know unless we try. Please, Turner." She took his hands in hers to pull him up, aware of the strength still present in his grip, and how his eyes looked at her.

"If that's what you want to do, all right. We'll give it a try."

They stood outside the shelter, enveloped in the heat that baked down upon them oven-like, but her skin prickled with a nervous wave of cold as she unbuttoned the front of her denims and watched him do the same, drawing them off slowly, along with his socks and shirt until he stood before her clad only in a pair of dark navy blue slim fitting briefs, waiting for her offering to the end of the rope.

Her shirt came first, exposing her, now that she thought about it, too skimpy, too sheer bra. The denims came next, leaving her with nothing but a snug bikini bottom between her and total nakedness. She added her clothes to the pile. What had they wanted the clothes for?

Her mind snapped back to the real problem at hand. "My grandma taught me how to do those braided cloth throw rugs made from material remnants. They were rugged and they lasted." She gathered the clothing up, and using his knife, began the process of ripping and tearing the material into long strips, twisting and braiding them into a short coil of rope. The knots tying her handmade length of rope to the other one would be boy scout simple and secure, if only she could keep her mind on what her fingers were doing and not on the firmly muscled, slim man who stood only inches from her, waiting, awaiting the results of her experiment.

"I'm ready," she announced and handed him the new rope.

"We'll see." He took it and entered the shack, crawling on all fours to a spot just inside the mine's opening. He dropped the cup over the side, creeping closer himself, and holding the rope out at arm's length when there was no more rope to lower.

"Please be careful," she warned him when he would have inched yet closer to the crumbling incline leading to the main shaft.

"Hold onto me."

She did so, gripping the ground with her knees and feet and toes, and holding onto his waist and hips with everything else. "Don't get any closer...please don't." She could feel the hysteria rising in her breast. "The ground around there isn't safe."

As if to attest to that, a few inches around the edge tumbled down the incline and into the pit without warning, and in response Honey dug her nails into the flesh of his legs, holding onto them for dear life as she had not been able to hang onto Daryl.

"Let me go, Honeysuckle. I'm coming out." He must have understood her fears, for though his thighs still held the marks from her nails, he made no mention of it, but backed out of the mouth of the mine, careful to keep the rope tightly wound around his wrist.

"Look at this! Feel it! Feel it!" She shouted to him as they drew the rope up and out of the hole.

"It's wet." He touched the material of a shirt to his lips, incredulously disbelieving what his eyes and fingers and her excited "I told you so's" told him to be true.

"It *is* wet." Her jubilation was missing from his statement. "But it won't do us a lot of good as it is. I was as close as I dared to get to the edge and I was holding the rope out at arm's length. True, the rope is wet, but we're going to need some of that length to tie a canteen off and bring it up safely once it's filled. And to have it filled, we have to be able to lower it into...not just touching...the water."

"Don't give up!" She hurled her faith at him like a curse. She had too much to live for to give up and wait to die. She spent the next half hour, despite his protests, tearing their sleeping bag and moon blanket to shreds, and weaving the nylon and plastic and foil into a complicated macrame of several feet in length.

"Give it to me." He snatched the weaving from her hands and tied a cup to the bottom of it. "Now fill it with sand."

"What?" The effects of too much sand and sun and too little water? She blinked up at him, not comprehending what he wanted her to do.

"Never mind." He filled the cup with sand with a sort of grim satisfaction and watched as, held out at arms length and swayed back and forth, the weaving began to unravel and snap and finally separated altogether with a light tug from his hands, dropping the cup to the ground.

"If it won't hold together very well up here, how is it going to hold up with a canteen full of water and gravity pulling on one end, and us and the weight of the rope pulling on the other?" He took her shoulders in his hands, lightly shaking her to get his point across. "I know you don't want to believe it; I know you have this unsquashable hope, you're an idealist; you have been about everything since the first day. But you're going to have to be realistic about this if you aren't about anything else. You're going to have to see this situation how it *is*, and not how you'd like it to be or how you wish it were. We do not have enough rope to get the water out. We have no other alternative but to wait."

"This is one of those things you're writing off as impossible?"

He released her arms, as if the effort to keep them there was too great. "It tops a long list that's grown steadily longer since I came back home. . . ." He let the word trail off. "Home. Why I would still have a love for a place that's never brought me any happiness I will never understand. The only impossibilities I've ever encountered that I couldn't overcome with hard work and perseverance have been here in Pahrump."

He poured the last of the water into one cup. "Here's to our rescue; may it be soon so that I can leave this land of impossible things and get back to my own world where everything I want is possible."

"You first." She pushed the proffered cup back to him, unwilling, as thirsty as she was to drink to his bitter toast and thus will him away and out of her life.

"Here." He insisted. "Finish it. It's all we've got."

The half cup of water wouldn't make much of a difference in how thirsty she would be afterwards, she had learned that in their several days of rationing, but ridiculous as it sounded, the thought of touching that water to her lips and drinking to the defeat of his dreams was more than she could take. But to explain that to him was more than she could do. She pretended to drink a little to satisfy him.

He ripped the cup from her hands and mouth, looking for a second like he might throw it. "If you're so damned eager to join your husband, there are easier and less painful ways to do it than dying of thirst. You can avoid life and living if you want to, but don't you dare make me the one who takes it from you. Now drink this, because I won't!"

"No. Stop it, Turner."

"Stop? I haven't started." He set the cup to her mouth in determination and poured, spilling half the water onto her partially bare breasts, dividing the rest between her mouth and nose until she coughed and struggled in his grasp.

Couldn't he understand that she didn't want to drink to him leaving her? Didn't he know how much he had come to mean to her in the past few weeks...the past few days? Didn't he understand how hard it had been for her to become one of his "impossibilities," and didn't he know that she no longer wanted to be one of them? The battle she had won against their desires brought her no joy. She stopped struggling in his arms.

"I won't drink to you leaving, but I will drink with you if you stop taunting me about a past I can do nothing about, and hold me for right now."

At his almost imperceptible nod, she tasted the water and passed the remaining drops to him, shrugging herself out of the rest of her clothes as he finished the water. There might not be another chance for them; if this was wrong, then let it be so, she would be answerable for her actions later. For now, there was no room for tomorrow's regrets and today's inhibitions.

"What are you doing?" He didn't know whether to accuse or wonder.

"Something I should probably have done before now." She crouched down beside him and pulled the briefs from his hips, keeping her eyes on them as they dropped down past his knees and to his ankles. She lifted each foot and removed the last vestige of his clothing.

"You can't do this because you feel sorry for me or guilty or desperate or whatever it is that you're feeling. I don't want that from you."

She kissed his knees which, in her crouching position, were at her eye level. "I don't feel sorry for you. I feel sorry for myself for being the way that I am, for wanting my cake and eat it too, for not being able to give you freely everything I've wanted to give you for weeks now." She ran her hands up from his knees to rest them on his hips. "This isn't charity . . . or if it is, it's a charity to me, not you."

"This isn't one of those times you'll regret what you're doing mid-way and stop is it?" He asked her hoarsely.

"I know what I'm doing, if that's what you want to know. I'm showing you that there's at least one thing you've been wrong about. You'll go back to Reno with one less impossibility on your long list."

He gave her no other objection as she made her way from his knees to his mouth, clinging to him as if everything depended on it once she got there.

"My God, did I die and go to heaven or is this another of my dreams?" He asked her when she released him long enough to speak.

"Neither. I'm here . . . I'm real."

"No you aren't," he denied. "Nothing this good could be real. You are a fantasy, Honeysuckle, my wild flower, a last beautiful mirage granted to me by the Gods who govern this damned impossible desert."

"I'm no mirage. Do I feel like one?" She pressed her body closer to his, daring him, speaking the heretofore silent and often denied wish aloud.

"You feel . . . exquisite." He complied with her desire, caressing her pale, rounded breasts, free of all covering but his ceaselessly moving hands that touched her here and there until she thought she would go mad with the wanting of him, until she thought nothing could feel so excruciatingly good, until he explored the rest of her with all the speed of a desert tortoise.

This was nothing like anything she had ever experienced before. She had been married, and the thought flashed in her mind that the mechanics had to be the same, and yet . . . Her lips parted, calling his name, willing him to come to her. She arched her hips to find him, to touch the man who approached his love making as he did all else, with an aggressive, dynamic intensity that was compelling. There was no one and nothing like him, and she longed to possess him for her own, to have him possess her completely, as completely as he wanted . . . anything he wanted . . .

"I want you so much." She whispered the entreaty.

"Do you?" There was only a small bit of controlled, logical sanity behind his question. "Tell me, even if it isn't true . . . tell me it's *my* hands that you feel on your skin when I touch you; tell me it's *my* body you need to feel within yours; tell me it's *me* you'll be thinking of when I take you with me to that place in loving where time stands still. Tell me for God's sake that you love me!"

She looked up at him with passion darkened eyes and reached for him, answering him with her body, tempting him with her nearness until with a half struggled sound he took her, loving her with all that there was of him until the sun itself seemed a pale, cold thing compared to the fire that they radiated together.

"Yes, yes, yes." She spoke to him at last. "It's you, only you, Turner," she cried out to him as he completed their union. She silently prayed it was true.

CHAPTER TWELVE

THE SUN DRIED the moisture on their skins, as it dried
the fountain of lovely things they had said and done to
one another. A moment where time stands still he had
promised her, and delivered; a world for them alone. It
had been so for her. She glanced at him out of the corner
of her eye. He lay as still as she, as if moving might
shatter what was left of the magic. How did he feel?
What did he feel? She longed to ask him, but did not,
afraid should he ask the same questions of her.

"Are you thirsty?" She uncurled her fingers from his
and, with her back to him, re-clothed herself in the bra
and panties that lay beside them in the sand. "Because
if you are, I think we may be able to get at that water.
I have an idea."

There was a safety in dealing with the necessities of
life.

"I was thinking..." She continued: "I was thinking
that we don't need five more feet of *rope* to get the water;

we need five more feet, if that, of anything. *You* couldn't reach it because you couldn't get close enough to the shaft without sliding down the incline or putting so much weight on the edge that it crumbled. If it did crumble or you started to slide, *I* might not be able to hold *you*. Do you follow me?"

He wore his nakedness nonchalantly, dressing as though his thoughts were totally absorbed with the problem she had posed for him. She squelched her desire to make him think of other things. There wasn't time for that now.

"I follow you all right, but I don't like where you're going." He dressed, speaking to her all the while. "Or to put it bluntly, I don't like where you think I'm going to allow you to go. If you think I'm going to let you go down in that shaft, by whatever means, after all that's happened..." He alluded to their lovemaking and more. "...you're sadly mistaken."

"But you could hold me where I couldn't hold you... you could pull me back if... if the ground did give way. I must weigh fifty pounds less than you do. That in itself would increase my chances. What other choice do we have? How long do you think we can go without water? We haven't had more than a few drops today and we've been on really short rations for a couple of days before this."

"Indian and the others could very well come today. They will have missed us by now." He protested.

"Are you willing to gamble your life on the hope that they will?"

He turned the tables on her argument. "Are you willing to gamble your life on the fear that they won't? We're desperate, but not that desperate yet, I hope."

She put her hand on his arm, feeling the firm muscles there. "You could hold my weight, I feel sure of it. I *know* you could hold me today, but what about tomorrow or the day after if something goes wrong and they still haven't come? What if we've had no water or food by then? Will you still be as strong when we've no choice but to gamble?"

He looked out over the horizon, willing someone from town, someone from anywhere to be there. But there was no one there. "I don't like it, but you have a point that I can't logically argue with. If you're bound and determined to make me responsible for your life, then let it be when I am at my best." He added an appendix: "And I think it's time I found Indian's lucky hat. I'm going to need it, that is, if you haven't thrown away our luck along with your good sense."

"I haven't done either, and I trust you, so let's do it."

The wooden shack walls rattled when they entered, the slightest vibration enough to shake them; but it wasn't the solidity of the mining shack they worried about, but the mine itself underneath.

"Are you all right?" Turner put a large hand around her wrist as they entered the dark opening, and she held it willingly for support. This was necessary . . . she reminded herself of it.

"Yes. Why don't I get into position first with you holding onto my feet. That way I can be free to use my hands to lower the rope and bring the water up." So brightly said, so easy. It would take less than ten minutes from beginning to end. She was confident they would be drinking the water from below within a quarter of an hour. That was why she had insisted he go along with her idea. Why then was her heart jackhammering away in her breast, her eyes filled with an irrational fear that she knew he would be able to see if he looked? She lowered herself quickly to the mine floor to avoid that possibility and took the end of the rope he offered with its denim and shirt additions and the canteen attached to the end.

The ground was littered with sharp stones that scratched her stomach as she slithered along, snakelike but she wasn't mindful of that, all her concentration centered on the sharp incline just ahead of her. She reached the point Turner had stopped at and went on, so slowly that everything seemed to be moving in half time, a slow-motion study in tense utter fear that, try as she would, she was having less and less control over, the closer she came to that crumbling edge.

"Turner, wait!" She trembled violently and bit her lip before she could go on.

"We can go back any time, Honeysuckle," he called to her, using the at first hated pet name. It comforted her now; it gave her strength.

"No. I . . . I just wanted you to make sure you had a good hold on me when I started down the incline. I wouldn't want to start sliding. . . ."

"The only way you'll start sliding is if you take me along with you, and I'm not going anywhere, so don't worry." His fingers bit into the flesh of her calves reassuringly as she lowered the canteen the few feet that was left on the incline and over the edge, scooting forward herself until her body from the hips up was pointed down, weightless, held from the hole below only by Turner's hold on the rest of her.

Foot by foot the canteen dropped, past the rotted shoring and jagged outcroppings of rock she knew must be there and could visualize in her mind's eye, into the darkness that shrouded the water below. Her concentration complete, she did not see the tiny grains of sand filter down from the edge in the darkness until her incline gave way from underneath, whatever supports had held it there torn away, forced down by gravity and her weight, taking all the earth from her waist up with it, plunging down and still down with sickening speed. She felt his hands tighten and heard herself scream at the same time, felt his muscles strain to pull her back . . .

Only later as she lay ever so still, ever so quiet, did she become aware of what must have happened when he braced himself against the support beams of the room to hold her, wooden beams even less stable than the mine itself, exposed to the harsh elements without protection for too long. The mining shack had collapsed.

The shaft was totally dark, she could see down into it now, most of the incline eaten away to reveal how large a shaft it really was, or she could have seen down into it if there had been enough light. As it was, there was only enough illumination for her to see how precarious her position was, to see that she was hanging from death's door only by her legs. She could not tell precisely what the bottom of the shaft looked like, or see what was down there. She was glad of that.

Minute particles of debris continued to drop from time to time, making ever so tiny splashes in the water far below. She'd make a large splash in more ways than one when her portion of the mine fell in. Turner would have to close the mines then, or at least see to it that Charlene would, if she as well as Daryl fell victim to their dangers. After what she had shared with Turner, surely he would do that for her ... when he was found. She had faith he would be found ... and she would be found, in one place or another.

It was a soap opera scenario, the mines being closed down only after claiming the life of the brave, handsome rescue team leader and his grieving widow some eighteen months later. She worked out several scenes, complete with dialogue and scene changes to pass the time, discovering as she went along that she didn't like the reality of martyrdom as much as she'd liked the concept of it. Furthermore, since meeting Turner, she had ceased to be either unhappy or grieving: confused at times, agitated and sometimes furious, certainly, but not grief-stricken. She'd have to rewrite the scenario.

She toyed with the idea of having him close the mines in gratitude after rescuing her, and that one had more appeal, but she could think of no reason in the world why Charlene would close them for that reason. She would probably not appreciate all that they had become to each other. Perhaps the mines wouldn't be closed ... but at least he would rescue her. It was a thought she could live with, and she could almost hear the scritch-scratching of him digging down to her as she fell into a daze.

Honey shivered and tried to curl up for warmth so she could sleep. The cold that gnawed at her bones was a real thing, the pounding in her head from lying head down too painful to allow her any real rest. All of it, the cold and the pain and the fear becoming part of a waking and sleeping nightmare from which there was no escape.

The scenarios on which she had passed the time during her waking hours had taken over her dreams, distorted, merging into two sides that tried equally hard to tear her apart. Daryl and the love she had once felt for him and the shaft and the cold and the nothingness, pulling her from one side. Turner and sunlight and warmth and the love she felt for him pulling her on the other. She had no control over who won and who lost, as though she was still undecided as to whom the final victor should be.

"We're close. I see her feet," an ecstatic voice cried and the digging became more careful. "Please, God, let her be alive and I swear on all that's holy these mines will be closed if I have to fill them in with a teaspoon."

Honey heard the words in a fog of half-dream, half-consciousness that were both clothed in a like darkness. It was Turner! She recognized his voice, and with all her being she wanted to feel his arms around her again. She wanted nothing more than to leave this place and live in the land of the living again with him.

"I'm sorry," she cried out in apology to someone long gone, someone who would not, if he had words to speak, deny her the love she had found. But there were no words, only the terrible dreams that had become a part of her reality, the cold and the dark and the hands that she could feel pulling her through the choking blackness of earth and mine shaft when she wanted no more of that place.

"No!" she screamed out with what voice she had left, fighting the hands, fighting the battle with death. She could not join Daryl in such a place. She belonged somewhere else, with someone else. "No! Daryl...no!"

Teresa gave a startled look and helped Pauline wrap her in a prewarmed blanket. All she heard, dimly was Teresa's voice.

"She does love you," Teresa insisted. "I know her,

and we've talked about it a little. I know she loves you."

"Perhaps as much as she was able . . ."

The darkness receded from her mind and from her eyes, blessedly proving false her worst fears that she would still be inside the mine, that Turner was not out there somewhere, that she was dead or he was, and she'd never be able to tell him how wrong she'd been, never be able to say . . . She moved her head to one side, trying to figure out where she was if not in the mine.

Her room at home, of course. She looked around the four walls slowly, conscious for the first time how much of her life had been wasted here, how foreign she felt here now. Wherever she belonged, she knew it was not here in this museum of a house with its kindly but oppressive curator who didn't want anything or anyone new added to mar the collection of her memories. Honey didn't see herself a souvenir of the past any more.

The floor felt odd under her feet, and her head swam when she sat up, but she was all in one piece, which was more than she had expected, and she was determined to find Turner to see if he was as well.

"I'm glad you're here; saves me the trouble of finding you. Where is Turner?" she demanded of Indian before he had time to step inside and bring Gerry and Teresa with him. "I haven't seen him since the cave-in and I want to know where he is."

Indian's face broke into one of the broadest smiles she had ever seen there, and he mumbled a few words in a language she did not understand. "You stay here. I will find him."

"Find him?" She questioned Indian but he slipped out the door before she could elicit an answer. "Gerry? Where is he? He's all right?"

"Yes, he's fine, in better shape than you." Gerry manhandled her back to the bed. *"You've* got a couple of cracked ribs and some pretty wild bruises. He's just got a few scratches."

"Then where is he? How long have I been here?" She had the feeling something was wrong, but she couldn't

put a finger on what it was, and Gerry and Teresa seemed
in no mind to enlighten her.

"We got you back last night, and he was here then,
but he had to leave to make some calls," Teresa explained
uncomfortably. "From what I was able to overhear, he
threw his weight around pretty well, got the presentation
postponed because of emergency circumstances and had
Charlene fly back with a group of V.I.P.'s to look at the
mine you were in. They flew over in a helicopter, the
whole bit. You both made the papers. I believe he's
going back to Reno today to make the presentation and
the recommendations himself."

Pauline had come in while Teresa was speaking, carrying a cup of soup and a thermometer. "I'm sure he'll
stop in and see you before he goes, dear. Indian said you
were awake and asking about him. It's just that he has
so much to do before he leaves."

"When is he leaving?" She looked from face to face
for answers.

The door opened again and the rest of them vanished
as fast as possible as Turner and Charlene came in. The
crisply pressed, expensive business suit was back, along
with the briefcase and the professional air that came with
it. The polished, unemotional man who had worn it to
town was back too, clean shaven, his mahogany dark
hair styled neither to hide or to accent the few flecks of
silver at his temples. Here was a man sure of what and
who he was, hard perhaps, efficient certainly. He did not
look to be the type to succumb to the pressure of what
he might like to do, over what he knew was right to do.
If he said close the mines, they would be closed; no one
would doubt his impartiality. And in case they needed
further proof, Charlene stood at his elbow, her pale cream
suit as professional looking and as icy aloof as she.

"Honey?" His eyes took in the pallor of her face and
the large questioning eyes. "How do you feel? I hear
you're going to be fine."

"Yes...fine." She heard herself repeat. "You're
leaving?"

"The job's done to all intents and purposes. As I'm sure someone has told you, we've had reporters and officials out looking at...your mine and several others all day." He glanced securely at Charlene. "We're going to recommend closure for all of them, and I don't think we'll have too much trouble getting it."

"Bad business having a high B.L.M. official involved in a mine cave-in accident after coming to see if the mines are safe or not," Charlene interjected dryly. "I'd say it's in the bag."

"Thank you." She said it stiffly, directing her gratitude to them both.

"It was what you wanted." He spoke very softly. "It was the least I could do."

"For services rendered." She whispered the words to herself. "Will I be seeing you at all before you go?"

He checked his watch impatiently, as if he was wanting to be off, then turned to Charlene. "Why don't you check on our reservations while I say good-bye?"

She left them alone, sent on an errand that was in itself an answer to Honey's question. She tried to assimilate the knowledge and not allow it to affect her, as she had once tried not to feel the pain of losing Daryl. He was going home, to another world in which she was no part of.

"Will I see you again?" It was a particularly humiliating question to have to ask after what they had shared.

"I shouldn't think so." He crushed her small hope with a few well chosen words. "I...there's nothing for me to come back here for, and you aren't overly fond of the city."

"There could have been something for you to return to. I could have learned to like the city—if you were there."

He watched her sadly. "No. I thought so once, but I was wrong, and you were right all along. I don't belong here, and you won't belong anywhere else."

"So you were leaving without bothering to say good-bye?" She got up from the bed and walked stiffly to where he stood. Her chin trembled in spite of the lower lip she held in clenched teeth.

"We never really said hello though did we, Honey? It was all on the surface with us."

"Like shaking hands?" She was bitter and didn't care if he knew it.

"No!" He let the word slip out with more emotion than she had seen so far. "But it was far less than I thought it was. I could never touch the center of you . . . only the outside. You never let me see all of you, only what you couldn't hide. I'm not blaming you, Honey. But it's not enough for me."

There had to be a reason for this. A man just couldn't turn from fire to ice in the space of a day, could he? "Do you think this is good-bye . . . permanently then?" She tried to keep her voice light, but she might not have succeeded because he bent to kiss her cheek with more tenderness than he had shown up until then.

"Yes."

"Isn't there anything I can say to change your mind?" She knew there wasn't from the firm, unyielding set to his jaw, the bleak uncompromising look to his eyes, set in a face too still, looking as if it were made of ceramic, as if a well thrown word could break it into a thousand pieces, if only she could find the right word.

"No, Honey. Let it be. You've said all there is to say." He touched a strand of her hair, not allowing himself to get any closer. "Be happy, Honeysuckle."

He left immediately, not giving her so much as a last glimpse of his face, not taking a last glimpse of hers, which was probably just as well, for the tears she could no longer hold back fell in abundance.

"Honey? Are you in pain?" Teresa dropped the newspapers she'd come in with onto the bed and moved to place an arm about her shoulder. "Here, let me help you back to bed. Where's Turner?"

"Has he gone?" Another face appeared around the door.

Honey thought the very last person she wanted to see was Charlene. "Yes. He's gone."

Looking like she had gotten the information she wanted, Charlene gave a nod and put her hand on the door, then stopped and closed it instead. "I don't understand you," she said.

At least she wasn't the only one who felt like she'd been dropped in the twilight zone. Could it be that cool and collected Charlene had moments of uncertainty as well?

"The mines are going to be closed. We've all but guaranteed that. You have what you want. What more do you want?"

She spoke as if she'd been handed irrefutable proof of a fact Honey was no longer sure about at all. She seemed gracious and genuinely interested. Of course, she could afford to be gracious, Honey thought bitterly. Turner was going home with her. Why not be honest about it?

"What more do I want? I think, just once, I'd like to be able to keep the man I love. I seem to be cursed with losing them just as I've found them. Failing that, I think I'd just like to be left alone." Her voice cracked with the effort she made to control it and she put her hands over her face, hiding from a reality she could not bear to see, waiting the agonizing seconds for Charlene to go after the man she herself could not.

"What happened?" Teresa asked after Charlene had gone. "What did he say?"

She swallowed several times before she could get the words out. "He didn't say much of anything that made sense; only that he was going and we'd never see each other again...that it was better that way."

Debating with herself, Teresa was silent for a few seconds. "You know I'm your friend, you know I'm not meaning to be hard on you, but I've never lied to you either, and I have to ask: What did you expect him to do?"

"I don't follow you." Was everyone purposely bewildering her today?

"From everything Turner said, from everything we saw when we finally located you, the man all but killed himself trying to get you out. He set fire to the shack, to what was left of your supplies, to the backpack, everything he could get his hands on to signal someone. When we got there, he was shouting obscenities into that worthless radio and digging for you with his hands... with his hands, Honey. He wouldn't let anyone pull you out of there but him, and when he did get you out, all you could do was struggle to get away and call out Daryl's name. The man loves you, but that's a hard blow to take."

"But you don't understand... he doesn't understand. I didn't want Daryl, I wanted *him*." The events, the garbled dream pictures, the jumble of conflicting emotions came back to her, yet the decision she knew she had made in the end was as clear to her now as it had been that night. Turner had misunderstood. They all had misunderstood. She leapt from the bed, oblivious to the discomfort in her side, and threw open the closet, extracting dress clothes and a pair of long neglected high heel pumps.

"What *are* you doing?" Pauline fluttered into the room at Teresa's insistence, both equally confused.

"I'm going after him, all the way to Reno if I have to."

It was obvious to them all who *him* was.

"Good for you," Teresa cheered. "I thought I was going to have to knock some sense into that stubborn head of yours."

"What time does his plane leave?" She shot the question out, demanding an answer.

"Charlene said two o'clock." Teresa checked her watch. "Ye Gods, Honey, if you leave now, you'll have to hurry to make it. Get going!"

"She most certainly will not get going!!" Pauline found her voice at last. "She's not well."

"I'll never be well again if I let him go." Honey took Pauline's hand and squeezed it with love. None of this had been Pauline's fault. "I've got to go, but I'll be back if he'll come with me, and if he'll be as welcome here as you've made me these past months."

Pauline hugged her close and pushed her to the door, unable to say the words she wanted to hear just yet, but unwilling to force her to stay any longer. Honey thought she'd come around.

The thoughts of Pauline left her mind as she got behind the wheel of the Bronco, back now and repaired. The road from Pahrump through Mountain Springs to Las Vegas had never seemed so long or so endless, though she pushed the speedometer past seventy most of the way, cursing the slower cars ahead, and praying the highway patrol was elsewhere just this once.

The airport ahead at last, she snaked in and out of traffic, leaving the Bronco double parked, illegally, the keys in the ignition when a glance at the large wall clock in the terminal told her she had less than three minutes until his plane took off.

"Excuse me! Please excuse me!" She raced past tourists and porters and security guards and hare krishnas that crowded the terminal.

"Can I help you, miss?"

Honey arrived at the empty boarding area, strewn with newspapers and vending machine cups, empty candy and cigarette wrappers. But no Turner, no one in fact except a flight attendant who repeated her question.

"Can I help you?"

"Flight 316 to Reno..." She collected her wits and her breath. "Has it taken off yet?" Her eyes followed the stewardess' nod toward the jet that was just now airborne, seen through the building's large plexiglass windows.

"There it goes now."

Honey hugged her arms to her aching sides and let the stewardess go, her services no longer needed or wanted. She walked haltingly over to the nearest ticket counter.

"I want to buy a ticket for the next plane to Reno." She dug in her purse for the money, hopeful she had enough or could charge it if she didn't.

"So do I." A voice said behind her. "And I think I was in line first."

"Listen Mr. . . ." She looked over her shoulder, her eyes wide with disbelief. "Turner?" Without further thought, she threw herself into arms that should have been several thousand feet up by now, but which thankfully, unexplainably, wonderfully, were not.

"What are you doing here?" She muffled the words into his chest.

He moved them both out of the ticket line and out from under the curious eyes of the others in line. "What are you doing here?"

"I forgot to tell you something." She tightened her hold on him lest he slip away again. "I love you and I won't let you go, even if it means I have to go to Reno and camp out on your doorstep. I can't lose you."

He crushed her to him, trying to hold her as tight as he could without doing further damage to her ribs. "And I thought I'd lost you, but Charlene seemed to think I hadn't. I disagreed with her, I fought with her, I refused to discuss it with her, but I'd forgotten how devious the female mind can be," he teased. "I don't know how she did it, but I found myself bumped from this flight, and I find I have to go back to Pahrump for some important papers that she *accidentally* left behind."

"Charlene did all that?" Honey took back every nasty thing she'd ever thought or said about the woman.

"Was she right?" He looked at her steadily. "Is it true that you do love me? Because I can't share you, Honeysuckle. I'm not that generous. If that's an impossibility, let me know now and I'll get out of your life right now . . . at least I will on the next plane."

"You'll do no such thing." She pulled him to the comparative privacy of the waiting area and sat down on one of the benches to talk. "I have to let you know how things are, and I'm hoping you'll understand. I'm hoping that what I can give you is enough."

He joined her on the seat, waiting for her to speak.

"I loved Daryl . . . you know that, and a part of me always will. I can't forget he existed; I don't want to. He was a good and caring man and a wonderful husband."

She hurried on: "But that *was* a part of my life that happened a long time ago. It's over now. The girl who was married to and who loved him doesn't exist any more. She isn't me. I have lovely memories of her . . . and of him, all tucked away in mental photo albums. I may take them out to look at them once in a great while, but if nothing else, I learned in that mine that I want more from life than memories. I want more . . . more than just a mirage of love. I want someone more solid and real than that. I want . . . I love you."

She felt some of the tension leave his body and he took her hands. "I'm ńot perfect. I'm all too human sometimes and I'm too old to change now. You'd have to accept me as I am."

"There's only one thing I'd change, one thing I promise you, I will change. I'm going to make you stop believing in impossibilities, about Pahrump, about us, about everything."

He took her in his arms, kissing her passionately, thoroughly, much to the enjoyment of a curious group of onlookers.

"Turner . . ." she murmured, only inches from his mouth. "We *can't* do this here."

He kissed her again with determination. "You said there would be no more impossibilities for us, and Honey, this is only the beginning."

Second Chance at Love

WATCH FOR
6 NEW TITLES EVERY MONTH!

Second Chance at Love

____ 06148-4	THE STEELE HEART #52 Jocelyn Day	$1.75
____ 06422-X	UNTAMED DESIRE #53 Beth Brookes	$1.75
____ 06651-6	VENUS RISING #54 Michelle Roland	$1.75
____ 06595-1	SWEET VICTORY #55 Jena Hunt	$1.75
____ 06575-7	TOO NEAR THE SUN #56 Aimée Duvall	$1.75
____ 05625-1	MOURNING BRIDE #57 Lucia Curzon	$1.75
____ 06411-4	THE GOLDEN TOUCH #58 Robin James	$1.75
____ 06596-X	EMBRACED BY DESTINY #59 Simone Hadary	$1.75
____ 06660-5	TORN ASUNDER #60 Ann Cristy	$1.75
____ 06573-0	MIRAGE #61 Margie Michaels	$1.75
____ 06650-8	ON WINGS OF MAGIC #62 Susanna Collins	$1.75
____ 05816-5	DOUBLE DECEPTION #63 Amanda Troy	$1.75

WHAT READERS SAY ABOUT
SECOND CHANCE AT LOVE

"SECOND CHANCE AT LOVE is fantastic."
   —*J. L., Greenville, South Carolina**

"SECOND CHANCE AT LOVE has all the romance of the big novels."
   —*L. W., Oak Grove, Missouri**

"You deserve a standing ovation!"
   —*S. C., Birch Run, Michigan**

"Thank you for putting out this type of story. Love and passion have no time limits. I look forward to more of these good books."
   —*E. G., Huntsville, Alabama**

"Thank you for your excellent series of books. Our book stores receive their monthly selections between the second and third week of every month. Please believe me when I say they have a frantic female calling them every day until they get your books in."
   —*C. Y., Sacramento, California**

"I have become addicted to the SECOND CHANCE AT LOVE books...You can be very proud of these books....I look forward to them each month."
   —*D. A., Floral City, Florida**

"I have enjoyed every one of your SECOND CHANCE AT LOVE books. Reading them is like eating potato chips, once you start you just can't stop."
   —*L. S., Kenosha, Wisconsin**

"I consider your SECOND CHANCE AT LOVE books the best on the market."
   —*D. S., Redmond, Washington**

*Names and addresses available upon request